SABOTAGE ON THE SOLAR EXPRESS ◈

Praise for Adventures on Trains

'Wildly funny, with hairpin plot bends and inventive characters, this series is firmly on track to become a bestseller' *Daily Mail*

'Mysteries on trains . . . what's not to love? Perfect for the railhead in your life' Ross Montgomery, author of *The Midnight Guardians*

'A pacey and intensely satisfying mystery, boasting a sparkling golden age crime fiction sensibility despite its contemporary setting' *Guardian*

'Like *Murder on the Orient Express* but better. A terrific read!' Frank Cottrell-Boyce

'I have a station announcement: [M. G. Leonard and Sam Sedgman's] collaboration is a chuffing triumph!' *The Times* Children's Book of the Week

'A sup   mystery' Peter Bunzl, author of *Coghea*

'Ideal   ashioned
myste

Other books by M. G. Leonard and Sam Sedgman

Adventures on Trains series
The Highland Falcon Thief
Kidnap on the California Comet
Murder on the Safari Star
Danger at Dead Man's Pass

and coming soon
The Arctic Railway Assassin

Also available by M. G. Leonard
Beetle Boy
Beetle Queen
Battle of the Beetles
Twitch

Also available by Sam Sedgman
Epic Adventures

M. G. LEONARD & SAM SEDGMAN

SABOTAGE ON THE SOLAR EXPRESS ◈

Illustrated by
ELISA PAGANELLI

MACMILLAN CHILDREN'S BOOKS

Published 2022 by Macmillan Children's Books
an imprint of Pan Macmillan
The Smithson, 6 Briset Street, London EC1M 5NR
EU representative: Macmillan Publishers Ireland Ltd, 1st Floor,
The Liffey Trust Centre, 117–126 Sheriff Street Upper
Dublin 1, D01 YC43
Associated companies throughout the world
www.panmacmillan.com

ISBN 978-1-5290-7265-5

Text copyright © M. G. Leonard and Sam Sedgman 2022
Illustrations copyright © Elisa Paganelli 2022

The right of M. G. Leonard and Sam Sedgman and Elisa Paganelli to be
identified as the authors and illustrator of this work has been asserted by them
in accordance with the Copyright, Designs and Patents Act 1988.

1 3 5 7 9 8 6 4 2

A CIP catalogue record for this book is available from the British Library.

Printed and bound by CPI Group (UK) Ltd, Croydon CR0 4YY

MIX
Paper from
responsible sources
FSC® C116313

ROUTE OF THE SOLAR EXPRESS

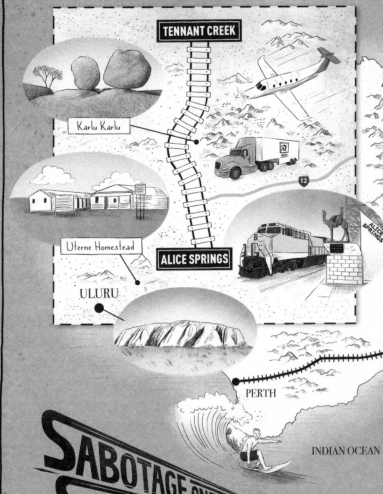

TENNANT CREEK

Karlu Karlu

Uterne Homestead

ULURU

ALICE SPRINGS

PERTH

INDIAN OCEAN

SABOTAGE ON THE ◇ SOLAR EXPRESS

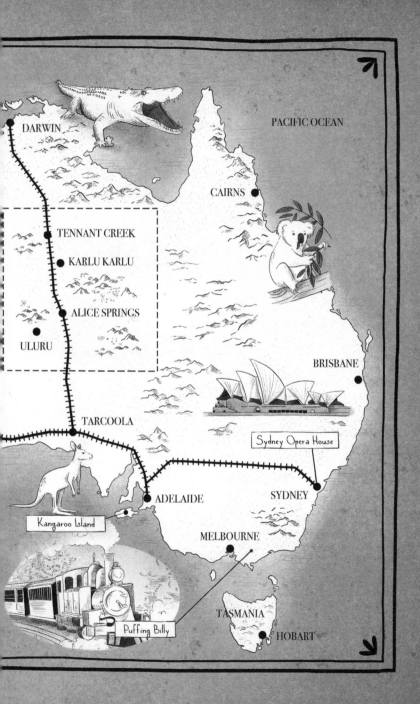

PACIFIC OCEAN

DARWIN

CAIRNS

TENNANT CREEK

KARLU KARLU

ALICE SPRINGS

ULURU

BRISBANE

TARCOOLA

Sydney Opera House

ADELAIDE

SYDNEY

Kangaroo Island

MELBOURNE

Puffing Billy

TASMANIA

HOBART

'We don't own the land. The land owns us.'

Aboriginal belief

CHAPTER ONE

AUSTRALIA

Life doesn't get better than this, Hal thought as he gazed out of the window at ox-blood earth sprouting with wiry shrubs pointing to a cobalt sky. He was sitting in a leather armchair, opposite his favourite uncle, in the Outback Explorer Lounge of The Ghan. He had a sketchbook on his lap and a pencil in his hand. He didn't need a mystery to solve. This trip was crime free, and he was having the best summer holiday ever.

They'd arrived in Australia four days ago, exploring the city of Adelaide while recovering from jet lag. Hal was surprised that the weather wasn't much warmer than it was back in Crewe, until Uncle Nat had explained that in Australia August was a winter month. They had a packed schedule of sightseeing and train excursions filling all three weeks of their trip. 'You'll be so busy having your mind blown by the beauty of Australia,' Uncle Nat had said, 'that there'll be no time for detecting.'

The day before they'd boarded The Ghan, Uncle Nat

had taken Hal on a ferry to Kangaroo Island. They had spotted dolphins and seals from the boat. The first page of Hal's sketchbook was covered with pictures of the koalas and kangaroos he had seen in the wildlife park, rescue animals saved from the recent bushfires.

Contrary to his dad's joke about everything in Australia being upside down and that Hal would have to walk on his hands to get about, the only thing that he'd found to be topsy-turvy was a *pie floater*, a delicious meat pie served face down in pea soup.

Yesterday, when they'd arrived on platform one of Adelaide's Parklands Terminal, they'd been met by a welcoming committee. The train crew of The Ghan, smartly turned out in Australian Akubra hats, were lined up in front of the impressively long silver train, waiting for their passengers. Emblazoned on each carriage was the train's name and the red insignia of a man riding a camel.

'Why a camel?' Hal had asked. 'Shouldn't it be a kangaroo?'

'The railway was built using camels,' Uncle Nat had replied. 'The name and insignia honours the Afghan camel drivers who first crossed Australia's scorching heartland.'

'*Are you ready for adventure?*' one of the crew had cried. They each introduced themselves, explaining what they did, so everyone knew who was looking after them and who was driving the train. The staff were proud to work on one of Australia's famous trains and their enthusiasm was infectious. One of them blew a whistle. '*All aboard The Ghan!*' they all shouted, before dispersing along the platform. It had made

Hal feel like an intrepid explorer about to set off on an epic journey.

Because The Ghan was the longest passenger train in the world, Hal and Uncle Nat hadn't had time to visit the twin scarlet locomotives before departure. The train was over three-quarters of a kilometre long, with more than thirty carriages, including a motorail carriage for cars being transported across Australia. Uncle Nat had reassured Hal that they'd see the locomotives when they arrived in Alice Springs, the next day.

Once on board the train, Hal found it was divided into areas. Their Gold Service tickets gave them access to the Outback Explorer Lounge, the Queen Adelaide Restaurant, and their compartment with two fold-away bunks.

As The Ghan trundled out of Adelaide, buildings became spaced out. Hal spotted some sheep, but then they were gone. The trees thinned, then disappeared altogether. Foliage faded and eventually there were more rocks than plants, and greater and greater expanses of rust-coloured earth. *It looks like Mars*, Hal thought as he drew the view.

As the train travelled north, Hal found it increasingly hard to contain his excitement. He'd barely slept last night in his bunk, despite the soothing motion of the train. He was journeying towards a momentous experience. The day after they arrived in Alice Springs, he and Uncle Nat would be some of the very first passengers *ever* to travel on the Solar Express.

The Solar Express was the winner of a global competition to create a futuristic train, for a planet facing the challenges of climate change. Famous tech entrepreneur August Reza had offered a big cash prize and the opportunity to work with his company, Reza Technologies, to build a prototype of the winning locomotive. The successful train designer was an Australian called Boaz Tudawali, who'd entered a hydrogen- and solar-powered hybrid engine. The Solar Express was his design. Hal had read about it in his dad's newspaper, then yelped with excitement when Uncle Nat had rung to tell him that August Reza had invited them to be guests on the maiden voyage of the Solar Express.

Hal chewed the end of his pencil, remembering his trip across America on the California Comet, when he'd first met August Reza and his daughter, Marianne. To begin with, Hal had got on well with Marianne. She drew comics and was

good at it, but he came to realize that drawing was the *only* thing they had in common. Marianne told lies easily and was used to getting her own way. Hal didn't trust her. But August hadn't mentioned his daughter in his invitation. Hal hoped that meant she wouldn't be coming on the Solar Express.

Taking his ruler from his pencil case, Hal drew a box around the picture he'd sketched of himself and Uncle Nat, sitting in front of the window of the carriage. He put a thought bubble above Uncle Nat, and inside he wrote: *Finally, a train journey with no crime.* He smiled as he added a vertical box to the left of the picture and inserted the caption: *The railway detectives were on The Ghan, travelling to Alice Springs.*

It was funny how drawing a box around a picture and adding a few words made it look like the beginning of a story.

He decided that if Marianne was coming on the Solar Express, he'd draw comics with her. He certainly didn't want to talk about what had happened the last time they'd met.

'Vast, isn't it?' said Uncle Nat, taking a sip from his coffee cup as he stared out of the window at the intensely blue sky. 'Do you know, Australia is wider than the moon.'

Hal's uncle was a travel writer and always had an interesting fact to share.

'Look, it's *Iron Man*.' He pointed to a sculpture beside the tracks.

The train manager's voice came through the speakers, telling them the *Iron Man* was created by the people who laid the one-millionth sleeper of this track, and Hal stared at the giant stick man carrying a concrete sleeper as they passed.

'Are you going to write about the Solar Express?' he asked his uncle.

'Of course! The Solar Express could revolutionize rail travel forever. What kind of a journalist would I be if I didn't write about it?'

'I don't believe it!' a woman exclaimed from a booth across the aisle. 'No one can be that lucky!'

Hal turned and saw a woman with red lipstick and cropped bleach-blonde hair sitting opposite a man in an open-necked, short-sleeved shirt. His tangled blond mop was scraped up in a top knot. A deck of cards lay on the table between them. The woman threw down her hand of cards, exclaiming loudly, 'Kenny Sparks, are you cheating?'

Kenny laughed, holding up his hands, displaying tattooed

6

biceps, as his female companion playfully grabbed at his shirt, searching for hidden cards. 'What can I say, Karleen? Lady Luck loves me.' A roguish grin spread across his stubbly face. 'Drinks are on you.'

Part of a neck tattoo was visible above Kenny's collar, and around his neck Hal noticed a gold necklace with a tiny pair of dangling dice. Without thinking, he started sketching the couple.

'One day your luck will run out,' Karleen said, shaking her head. Her hair was fixed with so much product it didn't move. 'One more hand.' She had an impish glint in her blue eyes as she gathered up the cards. 'Double or quits. Winner takes all.'

'Winner gets a steak dinner?' Kenny leaned forward with a questioning look.

'Deal,' Karleen replied, shuffling the cards.

Picking up his ruler, Hal drew a box around his sketch and, in a speech bubble above Kenny's head, he wrote: *Lady Luck loves me.*

'Hal,' Uncle Nat said. 'I think those are the MacDonnell Ranges.' He pointed.

On the horizon, Hal saw that the baked earth, peppered with pale, scrappy shrubs, rose into lumpen rock formations.

'*Ladies and gentlemen, if you look out your windows,*' said the train manager over the tannoy, '*you'll see we are about to cross the Finke River on a fifteen-span bridge.*'

Hal stared down at the custard-coloured water as The Ghan rolled over the narrow bridge. Most of the river was dry silt bed. On the far side, telegraph poles rose out of the ground

and a road curved to meet the track, running alongside it.

'*We are now approaching Alice Springs.*'

'We're here!' Hal said to Uncle Nat, who looked just as excited as he was.

CHAPTER TWO

ARRIVAL

The Ghan rolled into Alice Springs at a walking pace. Two open-topped people carriers scooted out from beside the hangar-like station, one driving towards the front of the train, and the other heading for the rear. A statue of an Afghan driver on a camel stood on the station concourse. A sign beside it read *Welcome to Alice Springs. The Heart. The Soul. The Centre.*

Hal descended the steps to the platform, thanking the attendant Nancy for taking care of them. Leaving the air-conditioned train was like sinking into a bath of hot air. As the powerful midday heat enveloped him, he winced, adjusting to the dazzling sunlight. 'Can we look at the locomotives now?' he asked Uncle Nat. 'I want to draw them in my sketchbook.'

'Yes. We'll grab our bags on the way back. The hotel isn't far from the station.'

They walked briskly beside the train for a long time, eventually passing a car park full of coaches, to reach the spot where the sturdy red locomotives had finally halted.

Hal dropped to the ground, sitting cross-legged in the dust, and set about drawing the face of the train.

He was finishing the outline of the insignia of the camel on the nose of the engine when he heard Uncle Nat suck in a breath of surprise. A black limousine, a Mercedes-Maybach, had stopped several metres away. The number plate said *REZA*.

The rear tinted window lowered, revealing the familiar, haughty face of a girl with a wavy blonde bob. She was wearing sunglasses. 'Playing in the dirt, Harrison?' she called out in her mid-Atlantic accent with a French twang. She chuckled. 'Why doesn't that surprise me?'

Hal jumped to his feet, brushing the dust from his legs. He wanted to reply with a cutting retort, but the heat of the Outback had scorched all clever words from his brain. To his frustration, he found himself giving a half-hearted wave and saying, 'Hi, Marianne.'

A familiar tall man, whose muscles threatened to bulge out of his grey suit, got out of the passenger seat and checked the area, before nodding and opening the rear door. Hal recognized him as Woody, the Rezas' bodyguard.

August Reza emerged from the vehicle. He was a wiry

man with a bald head and a hint of stubble. He wore clear-framed glasses, which darkened as he stood in the sunlight, an expensive-looking black T-shirt, and steel-blue suit trousers.

Uncle Nat walked towards the tech billionaire with his hand outstretched in greeting. 'August, what a pleasure! We weren't expecting to see you until tomorrow.'

The men greeted each other like old friends.

'We're going to meet with the designer of the Solar Express this afternoon,' said August. 'When you messaged ahead to say you were arriving today, I thought you might like to join us?' He looked at Hal. 'I'm excited for you to meet Boaz

Tudawali, Harrison. I think you'll like him.'

'But our bags . . .' Uncle Nat looked up the platform. 'We need to check into the hotel.'

'All taken care of.' August's fingers made ripples in the air, as if brushing these inconveniences away.

Uncle Nat gave Hal a questioning look, and Hal nodded. He could put up with Marianne's digs if it meant he got to meet the person who designed the Solar Express.

Clambering into the limousine, Hal found that the back of the car was a lounge with four luxury leather armchairs in pairs, facing each other, a miniature drinks tray between them. Marianne, dressed in knee-length shorts and a pale blue T-shirt, was sat in one of the rear chairs. She patted the seat beside her. Reluctantly Hal went and sat down next to her. Her hair had grown since the last time he'd seen her, but she didn't seem to have changed.

Lowering her sunglasses, so he could see her blue eyes, she whispered conspiratorially, 'There's something I need to talk to you about.'

'Me too,' Hal replied brightly, holding up his sketchbook. 'I've been drawing comics.'

'Is Mr Tudawali staying at the hotel?' Uncle Nat asked as he and August climbed in, sitting opposite them.

'No. He lives here,' August replied. 'Outside Alice Springs.'

Woody closed the doors, dropped into the passenger seat, and the limousine moved noiselessly away from the station.

'Is that why you're testing the Solar Express here?' Hal

asked, joining in with the adult conversation to avoid talking to Marianne.

'We built most of it here. Mr Tudawali is keen that the train serve the people of Australia, as well as America.'

The car turned on to the Stuart Highway, heading south, and the low rooftops of Alice Springs disappeared behind them.

'You must have had a lot of interesting entries to the competition,' Uncle Nat said.

'The prize was large enough to have got the whole world designing trains.' August shot him a mischievous smile.

'Any outlandish proposals?' Uncle Nat asked.

'Ha! Yes. Abu Dhabi University wanted to make a train with giant solar panels shaped like the sails of a ship. That was surprising. There was a wildly problematic entry from one of your fellow countrymen, a physics professor called Gregory Vulpes, who submitted a design for a nuclear-powered train. And – get this – there was an entry from a team in Denver led by one Gardenia Harmony-Chime that proposed we build a train from hemp and power it with vegetable oil!'

Marianne nudged Hal, trying to get his attention.

'What made you choose Mr Tudawali's design?' Hal asked, leaning forward.

'He was the obvious winner,' August replied. 'When you meet him, you'll understand why.'

'Is his train powered by sunlight?'

'Not quite.' August's eyes twinkled. 'His fuel system is ingenious. I think you're all going to be impressed.'

Marianne sighed loudly, letting them all know she was bored by their conversation.

'If you're not interested,' Hal said, quietly but curtly, 'why did you come?'

'I *am* interested,' Marianne whispered angrily, pulling off her sunglasses. 'It's just that Pop's being so secretive about this dumb train, and he won't listen to me.'

'About what?'

Marianne kept her voice low. 'Yesterday I landed at Alice Springs Airport, with Woody, and went straight to the hotel. Pop's got a suite of rooms. Mine is opposite the one he uses for business meetings . . .' She paused and frowned.

'What?'

'Forget it. I can see you're not interested.'

'Interested in what?'

She shook her head and looked out the window. 'It was probably nothing.'

'If it's nothing, then just tell me.'

'If I tell you,' Marianne said, glancing nervously at her dad and Uncle Nat, who were deep in conversation, 'you've got to hear me out.'

'OK.' Hal nodded.

'Yesterday I was coming out of my hotel room and I saw a hotel porter delivering a package for Pop. He knocked on the door opposite mine. There was no answer because Pop was down in the restaurant waiting for me. The porter put the package on the ground, slipped a card under the door and turned to leave. When he saw me standing in the corridor, he went stiff. He nodded at me, then hurried away.'

'What was in the package?'

'I brought it down to dinner. Pop opened it at the table. Inside was a detailed model of Stephenson's Rocket made from silver and gold, set on a wooden base with brass rail tracks, and sealed inside a glass case. People at the tables around us gasped at the sight of it. They were all staring. Hal, it's beautiful, like jewellery.'

'Who sent it?'

'That is the mystery.' Marianne leaned closer. 'When we got back to the rooms, Pop opened the card. It said: *Please accept this model of Stephenson's Rocket – the first locomotive – to commemorate your greatest venture, Reza's Rocket, creating the train of the future!*' She glanced at her father. 'He loves it. He did a press conference this morning sitting beside it. He even used the line from the card: *From the first locomotive to the train of the future.*'

'What's wrong with that?'

'Don't you think it's strange to give a valuable present to someone and not sign the card?' She didn't wait for his reply. 'I do. I wanted to know who the gift was from. I went looking for the hotel porter, the one I saw delivering it. When I asked in reception, they said no one matching his description worked for the hotel.' She widened her eyes meaningfully. 'And they said they hadn't received any packages for Mr Reza.'

'What did the porter look like?' Hal asked.

'He was taller than me, but not by much. He was slim, with a beard and there was silver in his hair. I only saw him for a minute, but I'd say he was about the same age as Pop. He was wearing a maroon porter's jacket.'

'Then he must work for the hotel.'

She gave him a scathing look. 'None of the porters has a beard. I've checked, and they're all much younger.'

'Did you tell your dad?'

'He didn't listen.' Marianne looked down at her hands. 'He loves the Rocket model. He said he didn't have time for my nonsense on this trip.'

Hal turned to look out of the car window, staring at a lone white cloud hovering in the azure sky like a spaceship. He knew Marianne made up stories to get attention. He reminded himself that he was not in Australia to play her games, but to ride on the Solar Express. 'It does sound odd,' he replied. 'But is it possible there's an explanation? Maybe the person who sent it forgot to sign the card and will get in touch.'

Marianne huffed, put her sunglasses back on and folded her arms across her chest.

Occasionally their limousine passed a lorry or a dusty pickup truck, but as crooked trees and weathered rocks came, then slipped by, the road became emptier. Eventually they turned off the highway on to a bumpy track. The car jerked and bounced as it rolled along over the potholes and stones. August put his hand on the drinks tray to stop the glasses rattling. 'We're approaching the Uterne Homestead – where Boaz lives.'

Hal saw a cluster of farm buildings, framed by clumps of twisted trees in the shadow of a high outcrop of rock. Beyond it was a sweeping plain on which cattle shifted in the distance.

The car pulled up in front of the single-storey house with a wide porch. A boy was sitting on the steps. He stood up. He was taller than Hal, probably a year or two older. He had broad shoulders and a forest of curly black hair fanning out around his brown face. He studied the limo with unreadable chestnut eyes, greeting them with a wry smile as they got out.

'Hi,' he said, lifting his chin, as if this visit was utterly unsurprising. Descending the steps, he wiped his palm on his torn blue jeans and extended it to shake August's hand. 'Nice to see you again, Mr Reza. Couldn't wait till tomorrow, eh?'

'I told your father I'd be dropping by. I hope that's OK?' August reached his arm out, indicating Hal and Marianne should come to him. 'I wanted to introduce you to my daughter, Marianne, and her friend Harrison Beck.'

'Great to meet ya.' The boy nodded at each of them.

Marianne replied with a condescending look.

'Hi.' Hal smiled, to make it clear that he wasn't like Marianne.

'Everyone, this is Boaz Tudawali,' said August Reza. 'The inventor of the Solar Express.'

CHAPTER THREE

HEAT

'You invented the Solar Express?' Marianne's mouth dropped open.

'Yup,' replied Boaz lazily.

'How old are you?' she demanded.

'Fourteen.'

'I'm thirteen,' she fired back.

'Good for you,' Boaz said, unblinking.

They stared at each other. Marianne broke the stare to scowl at her father. She obviously didn't like this surprise. She was an only child, and used to being the apple of her father's eye. For a second, Hal thought she was going to storm off back to the car.

To break the tension, he stepped forward, smiling warmly and extending his hand. 'It's great to meet you, Boaz.'

'Harrison, is it?'

'Hal – that's what my friends call me.' They shook hands. 'It must be amazing to design a train and then see it built. I can't wait to ride on it tomorrow.'

'Yeah.' Boaz chuckled at Hal's enthusiasm. 'I keep having to pinch myself. I didn't believe it at first, but it's real all right.'

'You are the three smartest children I've ever met,' August said proudly, ignoring Marianne's sulk. 'Together, you make quite a team. The future's in good hands, don't you think, Nathaniel?'

Boaz raised his eyebrows at this comment, and Hal blushed, but Marianne's expression was angry enough to have sunk ships.

A woman peeped round the doorway behind Boaz, then disappeared. Hal heard her call out, in a loud whisper, 'He's here!'

'Already?' a girl's voice replied. 'Where's JJ?'

'I thought you were looking after her! Vince! Vince? Have you got JJ?'

'What's going on?' rumbled a deep voice.

'He's here!'

'There you are, JJ!' said the girl. 'Put that *down*!'

'Come *on*. We mustn't keep him waiting.'

The Tudawali family came out of the house wearing polite smiles. A stocky man wearing a sandy-coloured, cotton rancher's jacket was carrying a little girl over his shoulders like a sack of potatoes. She was happily banging a toy digger against his head. Hal guessed this was JJ. A full-figured woman, with glowing brown skin and a centre parting in her hair, plucked the digger from JJ. She passed it to a shy-looking teenage girl with red-framed glasses, and hair scraped into a bun.

'Meet my family,' Boaz said. 'Ma, Pa, my sisters Allira and Jedda – we call her JJ.' He shielded his eyes from the sun, looking out across the land. 'Somewhere out there is my brother Koen.'

'I'm Vincent,' Boaz's dad said, putting JJ down. She immediately tottered away like a wind-up toy. Vincent had a salt-and-pepper beard and curly black hair like his son. Reaching out, he shook August and Uncle Nat's hand. 'Nice to see you again, Mr Reza.'

'I'm Marlee.' Boaz's mother greeted each of them warmly,

20

encouraging them onto the porch. 'Proud mother to this genius.' She pinched Boaz's cheek.

'Cut it out, Ma!' Boaz winced.

'Allira's a genius too,' Marlee said. 'She just hasn't found her *thing* yet – have you, Allira?'

'Ma!' Allira protested, rolling her eyes.

'Who's thirsty?' Marlee asked. 'Come inside. Get out of this heat.' She ushered them into an airy living room with high beams and weathered furniture. Jugs of iced water and fruit juice were waiting on the table, beside a tray of empty glasses.

'Tell me,' Uncle Nat said, sitting beside Vincent, 'is a homestead the same as a ranch?'

'Yes. We raise cattle and manage the land. Uterne Homestead is about a million acres.'

'A *million* acres!' Hal exclaimed.

'Australia is big,' Vincent said to Hal, 'The largest cattle station here is the size of Belgium.'

Marianne was clutching her glass of fruit juice and surveying the place like a detective studies a crime scene. 'Where did you design the Solar Express?' she asked Boaz. 'Your bedroom?'

'Nah. I share with Koen. He won't let me do my experiments in there. Says he doesn't want to get blown up in his sleep.'

'Your experiments?'

'Boaz's workshop is outside the house,' Marlee explained.

Boaz looked at Hal. 'Wanna see my lab?'

'Yes, please.' Hal stood up eagerly.

'It's just a shed,' Allira said. 'He burned it down last year.'

'I fixed it,' Boaz replied, getting to his feet.

'With help from Koen.' Allira looked at Marianne. 'Dad insists he have a fire extinguisher when he's doing experiments now.'

'It wasn't hard to make one,' Boaz said to Hal. 'They're just compressed air and water.'

Hal noticed Boaz's forearms were marked with scars.

Marianne stood up. 'I want to see it.' Her chin was jutting forward, challenging anyone to refuse her.

'Cool,' Boaz replied with a nod.

'Would you mind if I came?' Uncle Nat asked. 'I must admit to being curious about where the Solar Express was invented.'

'It's this way.'

Woody peeled away from the wall, walking closely behind Marianne. Her shoulders slumped as she realized he was going to follow her outside.

'You have a bodyguard?' Boaz asked Marianne, glancing over his shoulder at Woody as they passed through the kitchen and out of the back door.

Marianne nodded miserably. 'Pop's *very* protective.'

'That's awful, never being able to go for a walk on your own.'

'Yes. It is.' Marianne blinked, looking at Boaz as if seeing him for the first time.

'A person needs to walk.' He glanced sideways at her, a

hint of a kindness in his eyes. 'You know. Under the sky, with trees and birds. In nature. Alone.'

'Yes.' Marianne nodded vehemently.

They all followed Boaz across the yard, passing a tall barn filled with farm vehicles. Hal spotted a pair of quad bikes. 'Can you drive, Boaz?'

'Of course,' Boaz replied. 'We all pitch in, feeding and looking after the animals. Sometimes you have to drive miles to find them. Ma is a pilot so when she's in the air, she keeps an eye out for the herd and radios back their position if they've gone walkabout.'

Hal saw they were approaching a long, low shack with wooden double doors at the edge of the outbuildings. Solar panels were bolted to the corrugated iron roof, and pipes fed in and out of the chipped and scratched exterior walls, blackened in places by burns. He noticed a gaggle of metal cylinders standing in a shady lean-to outside.

'That's it.' Boaz pointed at the shack. 'That's my lab.'

JJ came tottering round the corner of the lab, dragging a lump-hammer behind her and giggling.

'JJ! Give it back!' A young man with arms like tree trunks appeared, running after her. He retrieved the hammer and tucked it into the belt of his shorts. 'Not a toy,' he said, waggling his finger.

'JJ make bang-bang,' she replied.

'No, JJ. No bang-bang.'

'Koen,' Boaz called his brother over. 'Come meet Marianne Reza, Hal and . . .' He paused, frowning at Uncle Nat.

'Nathaniel,' Uncle Nat said. 'I'm Hal's uncle, and this –' he gestured to the bodyguard – 'is Woody.'

JJ hugged Woody's leg in greeting. The bodyguard smiled awkwardly, patting her head.

'They're coming on the Solar Express tomorrow,' Boaz said to his older brother. 'I'm showing them the lab.'

'We're very proud of Boaz,' Koen said sombrely. 'But we're also very worried about the size of his head.' He tried to suppress a smile. 'It's growing alarmingly big, from all this attention. Dunking it in the water trough is the only way to shrink it.' Marianne giggled. 'If you notice . . .' He put his hands behind Boaz's head and motioned as if it were ballooning.

Boaz slapped his brother's hands away with a grunt, and Koen laughed.

'Mama has made lunch,' Boaz said gruffly. 'Go eat it.'

'Come on, little bilby.' Koen scooped JJ up with one arm. 'Nice to meet you all.' As he walked away, he called out, 'Remember – if Boaz gets a big head, you tell me, and I'll dunk it in the trough!'

'Brothers!' Boaz exclaimed as he yanked one of the double doors open. The lab was flooded with sunlight, and Hal saw that a trestle table had been pushed up against one of the walls, serving as a workbench. It was covered with scrap metal, plastic tubing, coils of wire and interesting-looking boxes. The walls had tools hanging from them, and beneath the workbench were canisters and shelves stuffed with chunks of wood, bricks and bits of machinery.

'You built this place yourself?' Hal said, stepping inside.

'Pa gave it to me for my tenth birthday, after I accidentally smashed the kitchen window. It's taken years to kit it out and turn it into a proper lab.'

'It's messy,' said Marianne, looking about.

'I know where everything is,' Boaz replied.

Hal pulled out his sketchbook and leaned it on the table-top. There was no way he was going to miss capturing a sketch of the place where a new train had been invented.

'Have you always wanted to be an inventor?' Marianne asked, running her finger along a hosepipe that fed into a tank full of bubbling liquid.

Boaz shrugged, as if he'd never thought about it. 'Guess

so. I've always wanted to know more – stuff that goes beyond where the school books stop, you know?'

'Where do you go to school?' Hal asked. They'd seen hardly any buildings on the two-hour drive to the Uterne Homestead.

'School of the Air,' Boaz replied.

'That's not a real school,' Marianne said disbelievingly.

'It's online schooling,' said Boaz. 'We're too far from Alice for me to go there and back every day. I get my lessons online. Thousands of kids living in remote parts of Australia do the same as me.' He picked up a spanner. 'And like I said, I taught myself the rest, using books and . . . trial and error.'

'Are your mum and dad good at science?' Hal asked.

'Ma is good with engines,' Boaz reflected. 'Pa's better with animals.' He shrugged. 'They're always telling us –' his voice became high as he impersonated his mother – 'when you find your *thing* – the *thing* that makes you happy and forget that time is passing – then you must do it, until the *thing* becomes your life's work.' He smiled. 'My *thing* is science.'

Uncle Nat drifted towards a metal structure that looked like a scuba diver's oxygen tank connected to a bubbling vat of liquid with tubes and cylinders. 'What's this?' he asked.

'My fuel-cell prototype for the Solar Express,' replied Boaz. 'It's a large version of one cell in the real thing, which has hundreds, but it convinced Mr Reza and won me the competition.'

'Is it . . . hydrogen-powered?' Uncle Nat asked.

'Yes.' Boaz looked impressed.

'How does it work?' Hal came over and peered into the tank.

'Like the engine in a car,' said Boaz. 'Except you put petrol in a car. The power made from burning the petrol drives the pistons and turns the wheels.'

'Like burning coal to heat water and make steam that drives the pistons of a train?' said Hal.

'Exactly,' said Boaz. 'But when petrol burns, it makes toxic gases like carbon dioxide.'

'The cause of climate change,' Marianne said.

'Right.' Boaz patted the fuel cell. 'But my engine doesn't use petrol. It uses hydrogen.'

'Hydrogen is a gas, isn't it?' Hal squinted as he tried to remember what he'd learned in chemistry.

'It's the lightest element in the universe,' Marianne said.

'I get power from the solar panels on the roof –' Boaz beckoned them over to a clear barrel of liquid – 'and run an electric current through water, which splits it into hydrogen and oxygen. This process is called electrolysis.' He pointed to some wires dangling either side of a dividing panel. Tiny bubbles sprouted from the wires and frothed to the surface. 'Oxygen appears on those wires, and hydrogen appears on those. The gas rises and –' he moved his finger to the two pipes collecting the gases – 'I capture and bottle it.' He tapped his shoe against the canister beneath the worktop. 'I have hydrogen in here.' Picking up a deflated balloon, Boaz fastened it to the spout of the cylinder. The valve let out a sigh as the balloon swelled. Knotting it, Boaz let it float up to the ceiling.

'One of its properties is that it's flammable.' He took a metre-long ignition stick, clicking a trigger at one end to ignite a flame at the other, and held it up to the balloon.

'Are you sure that's a good idea—'

Uncle Nat was cut off by a thunderous *BANG!*

Everyone ducked, and Marianne screamed as Woody threw himself at her, knocking her to the floor, covering her protectively as the balloon became a ball of fire.

The yellow flames rolled across the corrugated iron ceiling and vanished.

'Whoops!' Boaz chuckled. 'Should've warned you that was going to happen.'

Hal laughed.

'*Woody!*' Marianne shouted angrily as she got to her feet. '*You idiot!*' Her face was red. She looked round at them, then stormed out of the lab.

Looking downcast, Woody hurried after her.

'She needs to lighten up,' Boaz muttered.

Hal looked up at where the balloon had been floating moments before. 'That's what happens inside your fuel cell? Surely that's more dangerous than a car engine?'

'When petrol tanks catch fire they explode,' Boaz replied. 'Haven't you ever seen an action movie?'

'But if petrol spits out carbon dioxide when you burn it, what does hydrogen make?'

Boaz grinned as if he'd been waiting for this question. 'When hydrogen reacts with the oxygen in the fuel cell to make electricity, the exhaust is a compound called H_2O.'

'Water,' Uncle Nat said.

Boaz nodded. 'The hydrogen in my balloon, when it exploded, turned to water vapour in the air.' He pointed to the prototype engine. 'In my fuel cell, the exhaust water runs back into the electrolysis unit that creates the hydrogen.'

Hal's brain was fizzing like the tank in front of him. 'You can power an engine with hydrogen, made from water and solar power. Then when you burn hydrogen . . . it turns back into water? And nothing else? No pollution? No waste?'

'Science, man.' Boaz grinned. 'I love it.'

CHAPTER FOUR

THE ROCK

'I hear you've been blowing things up, Boaz.'

Hal turned as August entered the lab.

'Sorry, Mr Reza,' Boaz said, looking sheepish.

'It's Woody you should apologize to,' August replied with a chuckle. 'Has Boaz shown you his fuel-cell prototype?' he asked, and Hal nodded. 'It'll be the first RFC to power a vehicle of this size.' He rocked on to the balls of his feet, obviously excited.

'What does RFC mean?' Hal asked Boaz in a low voice.

'Regenerative Fuel Cell,' Boaz replied. 'I hadn't got to that bit yet.'

'Most machines require batteries that store power,' August said. 'For example, you charge the battery of an electric car while it's parked.' He held up his forefinger. 'But Boaz's fuel cell is a sealed loop.' He drew a circle in the air. 'Hydrogen burns, generating power, and the exhaust is water. Through a process of electrolysis, using Boaz's top-secret catalyst, this water becomes hydrogen again, and the oxygen – a harmless by-product – can be released. In this fuel cell, you only need to store hydrogen and water.'

'The solar panels on the roof of the train provide the electricity for the electrolysis,' Boaz added. 'The energy is totally clean. No battery required.'

'Are batteries bad?' Hal asked.

'They aren't good for the land,' Boaz replied. 'Batteries are made from lithium. Australia is one of the world's biggest lithium exporters. The mines cut through this country like deep wounds.' He shook his head. 'But we won't need to rely on lithium batteries if we can develop regenerative fuel cells. That's why I had to win Mr Reza's competition. If the best brains are working on RFCs, if that's where big money gets spent, then hydrogen power will be the future of transport.' He held his hands up. 'Why steal our energy from the earth when there's plenty available in water, air and sunshine?'

August nodded enthusiastically. 'The Solar Express will be the cleanest machine on the planet.'

Hal's skin tingled with excitement as he thought about tomorrow's journey. 'Why did you call it the Solar Express?' he asked. 'Surely it should be the *Hydrogen* Express?'

'Marketing,' August replied. 'In the 1930s, airships were an exciting new mode of transport. The enormous balloons that lifted the ships into the sky were filled with hydrogen.'

'Hydrogen is lighter than air,' Boaz said, 'but as you saw with my balloon, it's also highly flammable.'

'There was a grand airship, called the *Hindenburg*,' August

31

said. 'It made the trip from Europe to North America several times, but met with disaster in May 1937 when it burst into flames, dropping to the ground and killing thirty-five people.'

Hal thought of Boaz's exploding balloon and felt a chill. 'How did it catch fire?'

'No one's certain, but it's thought static electricity on the surface of the balloon was responsible for the ignition.' August sighed. 'The terrible disaster was broadcast on the news. People were horrified. It was the end of airships. No one wanted to fly in them. The accident created what is known as "the Hindenburg effect". People avoided hydrogen, despite it being a clean fuel that is easily managed safely, because of those awful images.' He shook his head. 'We can't call the train the Hydrogen Express without people thinking it's going to explode.'

'And Solar Express is a better name,' Boaz pointed out.

'Sorry to interrupt.' Marlee was at the door wearing a crisp, white, short-sleeve shirt and black trousers. 'I've come to say goodbye. I'm off to work. It was great to meet you. You're welcome at Uterne any time.'

'Boaz says you're a pilot,' Hal said.

'I am.' Marlee looked pleased that her son had been talking about her. 'I can fly you back to Alice if you like? There's room in the plane.'

Hal looked at Uncle Nat.

'Do go, if you want,' August said. 'I know you've yet to check in at the hotel. I need to talk to Boaz about tomorrow's press conference. Marianne and I will—'

'I want to go with Hal,' interrupted Marianne, who had appeared in the open doorway.

Woody was behind her. 'I will escort—'

'I want to go *on my own*,' Marianne said insistently.

August calmly met the fury of his daughter's glare. 'We had a deal, pickle,' he said quietly.

'If it helps,' Uncle Nat interjected, 'I can look after Marianne until you return to the hotel. It'll be nice for Hal and Marianne to catch up. Won't it, Hal?'

Hal felt obliged to nod.

Marianne beamed at him with gratitude, immediately making him feel guilty that he was only being polite. He wished Marianne didn't upset people so much.

'If you're sure?' August replied with a slight frown.

'It's no bother,' Uncle Nat reassured him. 'I'll take good care of her.'

'OK, Marianne, you can go with Nathaniel, but you'd better behave yourself, do you hear?'

'Yes, Pop. Thank you, Pop,' Marianne replied, all sweetness and smiles, but as August turned to Boaz, she stuck out her tongue at Woody, who shook his head and gave her a resigned smile.

'Anyone coming in the plane, follow me,' Marlee said, striding away.

'So long, Marianne,' Boaz called out as they hurried after Marlee. 'Later, Hal.'

There was a small aircraft parked on a patch of red dirt on the other side of the outbuildings. It had neat white wings, a red stripe along its belly, and a blue tip on its tail-fin. Above the four cabin windows were the words *Royal Flying Doctor Service*.

Hal hurried to keep pace with Marlee. 'Who are the flying doctors?'

'Parts of Australia are remote. Here in the Red Centre, especially so. You can be many hours' drive from a doctor or a hospital. That's bad news if you have an accident or become sick. The Royal Flying Doctor Service uses planes as a doctor's surgery and an ambulance rolled into one.' Walking to the plane's fuselage, she pulled down a curved door between the wing and the cockpit, which provided three steps up into the cabin. 'Our existence provides comfort and reassurance, as well as saving lives.' She waited for Uncle Nat and Marianne to catch them up. 'Hop in.'

Clambering into the aircraft, Hal's nostrils flared at the pungent smell of disinfectant. The cabin was compact. Uncle Nat had to stoop to come inside. There were three seats. Space for the

fourth was taken up by a blue vinyl stretcher strapped to the wall. A machine that looked like a heart monitor was clipped to the ceiling, wires and tubes dangling from it. The cabin was like a quirky ward in a tiny hospital.

'Strap yourselves in.' Marlee pulled the cabin door closed and climbed into the cockpit, putting on a headset.

Hal sat down next to Marianne, who looked unimpressed by the plane. Never having been in a light aircraft before, Hal felt a thrill of nerves that he tried not to show. Marlee flicked switches on the control panel and the four-pronged propellor spun into life. The plane vibrated and Hal clutched the sides of his seat.

They taxied away from Uterne Homestead on to a clear stretch of bald earth. Hal was pushed back into his seat as the rattling plane accelerated. He stared out of the small round window as Marlee adjusted the wing flaps and the plane pulled up. His stomach dropped as the earth fell away and

they climbed towards the bright blue sky.

Circling the ranch, they flew over a high rocky outcrop and levelled off, and as they headed towards the horizon, Hal relaxed his grip.

'Are we near Uluru?' Marianne asked Marlee.

'If you call three hundred kilometres near!' Marlee laughed.

'Oh.' Marianne looked disappointed. 'I thought we might be able to see it from up here.'

Marlee looked at her watch. 'I've got a little time.' She looked over her shoulder and winked. 'I think we could fit in a flyover.'

The plane tilted, banking in a graceful curve as they headed off in a new direction.

'What's Uluru?' Hal asked Uncle Nat.

'I can only tell you what the guidebooks say,' Uncle Nat replied. 'It's a giant sandstone rock taller than the Eiffel Tower and longer than seventy rugby pitches. The custodians of Uluru are the Anangu people, and they believe Uluru was made during the Dreamtime, by the creators of the Earth.' He looked at Marlee. 'How did I do?'

'Not bad.' She laughed. 'There are different stories that tell of how our ancestral spirits brought about Uluru.'

'Your ancestral spirits?' Marianne asked.

'We are all made from the earth and we will return to it,' said Marlee. 'The land holds the memory of our ancestors, the people who made us. That's why we raise our children to respect the land. Aboriginal people have a saying – we don't own land, the land owns us.'

Hal remembered what Boaz had said about the lithium mines cutting through the country like wounds, and understood why he'd made it his mission to make a hydrogen-powered train. He thought he should try and draw Uluru, and took out his sketchbook and pen so he was ready.

Uncle Nat was leaning forward and chatting to Marlee.

'How long have you been flying planes?'

'I've been a line pilot with the RFDS for eight years,' Marlee replied. 'I was training to be a nurse when I got a work placement with the flying doctors. By the end of my first day, I knew I wanted to be a part of their team. I was inspired by the pilots, and in my spare time I took flying lessons. My first job with the RFDS was as a nurse, but eventually I got my flying licence and made the transition to line pilot. I love it. Vince would rather I was around more, to help with the ranch, but he's proud of me. I'm making a difference to people's lives.' She paused, then called out, 'OK, everybody, look out of the windows.'

Hal felt the plane tilt. The right wing dipped, bringing the ground into view and, rising from the earth, he saw an enormous rock the size of a town.

'Look!' Marianne grabbed Hal's leg. 'Uluru.'

'Beautiful,' Uncle Nat said under his breath.

As the plane flew in a wide circle, the mammoth rock turned slowly beneath them. Hal attempted to capture an image of Uluru from above. Shadows danced across the ancient orange stone, mocking his pen's attempt to trap them on paper. He realized it would be difficult to capture a perfect

image of Uluru. It was as changeable as a living thing.

'It's glowing,' Marianne said with awe, 'like a colossal ruby on the sand.'

'I'm afraid we must head back to Alice now,' Marlee said, levelling the plane. 'I can't be late.'

'Thanks for bringing us, Mrs Tudawali,' Marianne said, gazing back at Uluru.

'Yes,' Hal agreed. 'Thank you.'

It was dusk when they landed in Alice Springs Airport. They waved their goodbyes to Marlee, and Uncle Nat hailed a taxi to the hotel.

'Pop won't be back for ages,' Marianne said, as she and Hal climbed into the back seat of the car. 'Do you want to see his model of the Rocket?'

Hal paused. He didn't want to get mixed up in one of Marianne's schemes.

'Look, you're probably right, there'll be a good explanation as to why the person didn't give their name on the card, but I'd feel better if you'd look at it.' Her voice took on a pleading tone. 'For Boaz and Pop?'

Hal nodded. 'OK.' He had to admit he was curious to see this mystery model train.

CHAPTER FIVE

THE INSIDER

The hotel was on the edge of Alice Springs beside a dry river called the Todd. By the time they had pulled up outside it, the sky was indigo, and the only thought on Hal's mind was *dinner*. He'd always imagined hotels to be tall buildings, but this one was wide and sprawling. The triangular roof above the main entrance was brightly lit, and the lobby was impressively cavernous. Inside, the floor and pillars were made of champagne-coloured marble, and structural silver sculptures hung like modern chandeliers from the high-vaulted ceiling. Uncle Nat headed to the long reception desk to check in.

Marianne pulled Hal onto a low sofa beside a grand piano. 'That man talking to your uncle is the hotel manager – and look, there's one of the porters.'

A young man in a maroon blazer came from behind the desk dragging Hal and Uncle Nat's suitcases.

'See?' she hissed. 'He looks eighteen years old, twenty at most. The man who delivered Pop's package was older than even the hotel manager.' She looked at Hal.

'What?'

'Get out your sketchbook and draw things,' Marianne said impatiently. 'Isn't that how you solve crimes?'

'But there hasn't been a crime!' Hal protested as he pulled out his sketchbook. It was easier to humour Marianne than argue with her. Taking the lid off his pen, he marked out the clean architectural lines of the lobby.

'*Yet*,' Marianne muttered. 'There hasn't been a crime *yet*.'

'You're going to have to keep quiet if you want me to draw,' Hal said, sketching in the figure of Uncle Nat, beside

the porter with the cases, and the hotel manager behind the desk. He smiled to himself as Marianne clamped her mouth shut.

An elderly gentleman with combed-back white hair came out of the lift, shuffling to the desk clutching his room keys, patiently waiting until the hotel manager had finished serving Uncle Nat. Hal added him in to the picture. 'What about that guy?' He nodded to the elderly gentleman. 'Was he the one who delivered the package?'

'Don't be an idiot.' Marianne scowled at Hal. 'He's too old! I told you, the delivery man had a beard.'

Moving away from the reception desk, Uncle Nat waved at them. 'Let's get our luggage into the room, and then we can see about dinner. I'm starving.'

Hal jumped up at the mention of food.

'Mr Bradshaw,' Marianne said, pushing in front of Hal. 'I was telling Hal about the Presidential Suite, where Pop and I are staying, and how it has a private swimming pool. He's too shy to say, but he really wants to have a swim.'

'Oh!' Uncle Nat looked at Hal, who found he was speechless and blushing at Marianne's barefaced lie.

'Why don't you take your luggage to your room,' Marianne suggested, 'then come to the Presidential Suite? We'll order room service. You can eat, and Hal can swim.' She smiled sweetly.

'If that's what Hal wants,' Uncle Nat said, 'I don't mind.' Hal thought he caught a trace of amusement in his uncle's expression. 'I'll be along in ten minutes.' He followed the porter into the lift. 'I'll bring your swimming trunks, shall I, Hal?'

'What did you say that for?' Hal snapped after the lift doors had closed.

'Because I want to show you the Rocket model. If your uncle is with us, he'll tell Pop.' Marianne strode across the carpeted aisle of the lobby. 'Come on. The lift is in use. There are stairs this way.'

Hal reluctantly followed her, certain he'd made a mistake in agreeing to help her.

Marianne halted, grabbing for Hal's arm. 'Look!' She pointed through the open doorway of a function room. Rows of empty chairs were waiting for an audience. At the other end of the room was a low stage framed by vertical banners that read *Solar Express* above a logo of a blue sun. A table with three microphones positioned in front of three chairs stood in the middle of the platform. At the front of the table, in its glass case, was the shining model of Stephenson's Rocket. Even from this distance, Hal could see it was a work of art.

'This must be where they're holding the press conference tomorrow morning.' Marianne glanced over her shoulder to check the coast was clear, then dashed into the room. 'Quick.' She ran to the other end of the room, and Hal hurried after her. They both dropped to the ground as they heard voices. Marianne crawled to the right of the stage on all fours, and Hal joined her to hide behind a giant speaker. His stomach growled, and she put her finger to her lips.

'Um, excuse me,' a plummy British voice said from

43

the doorway. 'Is this the room for the Solar Express press conference? We were told we could come in and set up.' Hal saw that the speaker was dressed in a short-sleeved shirt and chinos, wore glasses, and had tousled hair. He was talking to a waitress, who pointed at the banners on the stage. 'Ah, yes, I see. May we go in?'

'Get in there, Tom.' A stocky woman in a purple vest and faded black jeans, her red hair plaited in pigtails, pushed past him carrying two heavy black bags. 'Don't mind us,' she said to the waitress. 'We're from World News.' She looked at Tom. 'We'll set up over there, left of stage. That way we'll get the banners in back of shot, and I'll have a decent angle on the table.' She walked over and dumped the bags on the ground with a grunt, then tilted her neck to stretch out her shoulders.

'Brilliant. Yes. My thoughts exactly,' Tom said, stumbling after her. 'Um, Kira, do you think I should wear the blue suit tomorrow, or the grey?'

'You're not the story, Tom. So long as you're dressed, I don't think it matters.' Kira pulled a tripod out of one of the bags and opened it out.

'August Reza usually wears grey,' Tom said, half to himself, 'so I should probably wear blue.'

'Hold this.' Kira lifted a camera from the bag, dumping it into Tom's arms.

'This is going to be my big break, Kira, I can feel it,' Tom said, awkwardly cradling the camera like a bachelor holding a baby. 'If this story gets syndicated around the world, then it'll be goodbye, World News . . . and hello, BBC.'

'Only if something interesting happens,' Kira said, as she tightened wheels and flipped down clips on the tripod. 'Anyway, what's wrong with World News?'

'I'm not made for travel,' Tom replied, as Kira took the camera from him and attached it to the tripod. 'When I set out to be a reporter, I thought I'd be working in a studio in London and occasionally standing outside the Houses of Parliament on a blustery day summarizing the goings-on in the House of Commons. I didn't think I'd end up in the Australian Outback reporting on the wild camel population.'

'We've all got dreams,' Kira said, fiddling with the settings on the camera. 'I'm a documentary filmmaker, but I also need to eat. I'm grateful that World News puts food on my table.' She handed him a microphone. 'Let's try a test shot.'

Tom stood up straight, ran his fingers through his hair and looked down the barrel of the camera. 'Good morning. I'm Tom Flinch for World News, and today we're in Alice Springs, Australia, where notorious tech billionaire August Reza is testing what he says is going to be the train of the future, the Solar Express.'

'*And* Francisco Silva,' a deep voice boomed from the back of the room, making Hal jump.

Tom and Kira swung around. A short, round man was standing in the doorway. He had a bushy beard, streaked with grey, and longish hair. He was a hairy man, with curls sprouting from the open neck of his blue shirt and making a fringe around his cuffs.

'You are quite right, Mr Silva, my apologies,' Tom said cheerily. 'I was speaking off the cuff, doing a test shot.'

'It's funny how people always forget my name.'

'Um, I didn't forget it. I . . .'

'It is *my* team of engineers that has built the Solar Express.' Francisco Silva strolled towards Tom. 'August loves to stage a press conference, throw a competition, wave money round, but it's me and my team that do the work.'

'That is so true.' Tom nodded sincerely. 'Has anyone ever taken the time to interview you, in depth, about your work?' He glanced at Kira. Hal noticed her touch a button on the camera. A red light came on.

Francisco shook his head. 'People are only ever interested in August.'

'I'm shocked!' Tom looked outraged. 'I know our viewers would be fascinated to find out more about the famous Reza and Silva partnership.'

'Silva and Reza.'

'Yes. Silva and Reza.' Tom's hand came to his chin as if an idea had just popped into his head. 'I don't suppose you could spare some time tomorrow morning, before the press conference? We could meet you here. I'd love to hear your thoughts on the Solar Express.'

'I'm giving a tour of the Solar Express to a retired Australian engine driver first thing, but afterwards . . .' He paused to consider Tom's proposition. 'It'd be nice to have my voice heard for once. August sure as hell never listens.'

'He doesn't?' Tom leaned forward.

'No. I don't think the Solar Express test run should be happening tomorrow.'

Hal's eyes widened, and he opened his sketchbook, laying it flat on the floor to draw the scene.

'Why not?'

'This is our first prototype. There's a lot that could go wrong. It's too early for passengers. I don't think the train will get more than a hundred metres out of the station.' He shook his head. 'Sure, we've got the loco working on test tracks, but it's never pulled carriages, and the automated driving system has glitches. The whole thing could be a major embarrassment for my team. We need more time before we go announcing we've solved the world's transport problems, but will August listen?' Tom and Kira shook their heads sympathetically.

Marianne's face was a picture of fury. Hal thought she might stand up and shout at Francisco Silva, but instead she took the pen from him, adding a speech bubble to his picture, above Francisco's head. Inside it she wrote *August doesn't listen to anyone*. Then she added a thought bubble above Tom Flinch's head: *This is a scoop!*

'I have a dinner to get to,' Francisco said. 'We're meeting Terrance Chang, from Chang Corp, and the Honourable Leslie Deane, Minister for Transport.'

'Are they travelling on the Solar Express tomorrow?' Tom scrambled to find his notebook and scribble this down.

'Yeah, we need to persuade Leslie Deane to support our application to lease land for clean hydrogen production.'

'What's the boss of the biggest mining and shipping

company in the Southern Hemisphere doing here?'

'August thinks he can persuade Mr Chang to power his ships with the Tudawali RFC.' Francisco snorted. 'I don't think he'll have much luck. Terrance Chang has a huge financial stake in the lithium-mining business. He's not going to be enthusiastic about competition.' He turned to leave. 'I'll do your interview. Meet me half an hour before the press conference. Oh, and tell reception when you've finished in here. They'll send someone to lock up the room.'

'Thank you, Mr Silva,' Tom called after the departing man. 'See you in the morning, sir. We'll be here.'

Once Francisco had gone, Tom looked at Kira and grinned. 'BBC, here I come.'

As the World News team left, Marianne whispered in Hal's ear. 'We've only got a few minutes before they come and lock the room. Come on.' She dashed on to the stage, with Hal right behind her.

'Go to the door and be lookout,' he said, slamming his sketchbook on the table in front of the Rocket model. 'I'll be as quick as I can.' His eyes were already registering the lines of the beautiful machine and translating them into rectangles and circles on the page.

'A porter's coming!' Marianne called out.

'I need more time,' Hal said, his hand working as fast as it could.

Marianne didn't reply, but a moment later he heard her talking to someone in the hall. 'Excuse me, where is the restroom? Thank you . . . Actually, could I ask you, what are the good tourist attractions in Alice Springs? For kids, I mean.'

Hal drew speedily as Marianne asked the porter question after question.

'Is it true that there are deadly spiders in Australia that hide in toilets? . . . Have any deadly spiders ever been found in this hotel? . . . What should I do if I find one? . . . Is it OK if I scream? . . . What if it bites me on the bottom? . . . Do you keep anti-venom in the hotel?'

When he was finished, Hal took a second to register the sheer beauty of the intricate machine in front of him, and then ran for the door. Slipping into the hallway behind the porter, he caught Marianne's eye and walked nonchalantly to the lift. She was at his side a moment later and they stepped into the lift together.

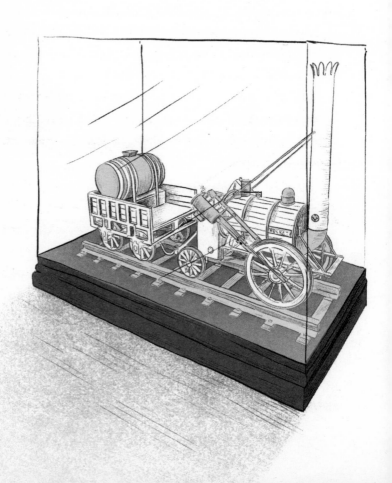

CHAPTER SIX

SPLASH

When Hal and Marianne arrived at the entrance to the Presidential Suite, they found Uncle Nat sitting on the floor reading a menu.

'Ah, there you are,' he said, getting to his feet. He looked at them enquiringly, waiting for them to explain where they'd been. Marianne opened her mouth, and before she could tell another lie, Hal spoke.

'We've been investigating.'

Uncle Nat nodded, unsurprised. 'Can I ask what?'

Dumbstruck that Hal had spilled the beans, Marianne stared at him.

'Uncle Nat and I work together,' Hal told her. 'If you want me to investigate who gave that model to your dad, and why, then my uncle needs to know everything too.'

Unsure, for once, of what to say, Marianne did a good impression of a goldfish.

'May I suggest we go inside and talk about this over dinner?' Uncle Nat said, holding up the menu. 'If you'd come along five minutes later, you'd have found me gnawing on my shoe.'

Pulling a key from her pocket, Marianne let them through a door into a semicircular vestibule. She pointed to a door. 'That's where Pop works, and where the porter left the package.' She glanced at Uncle Nat. His expression was unreadable. 'This is the lounge and the pool. We can call room service and eat in here. There's a table.'

As she opened the door, Hal gawped at the view. The room was the size of his school assembly hall. The left side was carpeted with a thick cream rug. On it was a semicircular leather sofa set before a giant screen with a games console. On the right side of the room was a kidney-shaped swimming pool sunk into a tiled floor, a separate jacuzzi, and a pair of loungers beside it. In the middle of the room was a ping-pong table.

'We can take the net off and bring those chairs over to eat.' Marianne pointed at four high-backed chairs against the wall.

'You can watch TV while you swim?' Hal was in awe.

'I like to swim to music,' Marianne said.

Hal saw there were speakers hanging from all four corners of the ceiling.

'Right, who wants what for dinner?' Uncle Nat had already found the phone and his finger was poised to dial reception.

'Can I have a Caesar salad and an orange juice?' Marianne said.

'Burger and chips with ketchup and an apple juice?' Uncle Nat asked Hal, who smiled and nodded. They'd travelled together a lot, and knew each other's likes and dislikes.

While Uncle Nat was ordering their food, Marianne took a pair of thick towelling robes from some hooks on the wall and handed one to Hal. 'Are you going to tell your uncle everything?' she asked in a low voice.

'Yes. You heard Francisco Silva downstairs.'

'You think he gave Pop the model?'

'I don't know about the model, but Francisco is definitely angry with your dad.'

'I knew it was him,' Marianne tutted angrily. 'He and Pop are always fighting.'

'I didn't say that. We don't know who the model is from. And it seems like a lovely gift. We can't jump to conclusions.'

'Who else could have sent it?'

'I don't know. What about that Terrance Chang man they were talking about? Francisco said he's heavily invested in the lithium-mining business.'

'Oh! You're right.'

'He has a motive for wanting the Solar Express to fail.'

'But why would he send Pop a gift?'

'I don't know what the Rocket model has got to do with any of this. That's why we need to talk to Uncle Nat.' Hal looked Marianne in the eye. 'Listen. I didn't believe you at first – about it being strange, and the mystery delivery man – but I do now. And if anyone is trying to mess up Boaz's train launch, then I want to stop them.'

'Me too.' Marianne smiled shyly.

There was a click as Uncle Nat put down the receiver.

'Food's on its way.' He took a chair and sat down at the ping-pong table. 'Right, let's hear what nefarious happenings have suddenly made you two thick as thieves.'

Hal brought over another two chairs while Marianne explained the strange gift of the model of Stephenson's Rocket, and how the man who had delivered it had vanished.

'The model is beautiful,' Hal said, opening his sketchbook and showing his uncle.

'Does it work?' Uncle Nat asked Marianne, who looked confused by the question. 'I mean, is there a switch that makes all the wheels and pistons move?'

'I don't think so.' Marianne shook her head. 'The case is sealed. It has a flat, wooden bottom and the glass is attached, so you can't open it. There aren't any switches on the outside.'

'Oh.' Uncle Nat frowned, looking at the drawing in Hal's sketchbook and then at his nephew. 'Did it look to you like it might work?'

Hal thought about this, and then nodded, pointing to his drawing. 'The wheels are a couple of millimetres above the track. They don't actually touch, so if there was some way of turning the engine on, they could rotate.'

'But it's sealed in a case. You can't turn it on,' Marianne said, staring at Hal's picture.

'Is there anything else you noticed about the model?' Hal asked his uncle. 'I know what Stephenson's Rocket looks like, but not well enough to know if there is anything strange about it.'

Uncle Nat shook his head. 'Not off the top of my head,

but we can easily get an image of the real thing.'

'You'll be able to take a closer look in the morning, at the press conference,' Marianne said. 'The model is going to be on stage with Pop. He loves it – says it's an iconic symbol of the Industrial Revolution, just like the Solar Express will be of the Green Revolution.'

'That's where we went,' Hal admitted. 'Marianne wanted to show me the model. But then we accidentally overheard a conversation between Francisco Silva and a news crew. Mr Silva said the test tomorrow shouldn't be happening. He seemed pretty cross with Mr Reza.'

Marianne nodded. 'Francisco and Pop argue about everything.'

'You mustn't worry,' Uncle Nat said, with a reassuring smile. 'Adults argue about things, but it doesn't mean they've fallen out. Business partners often disagree about the finer points of the project. Mr Silva may think the launch is too early, but he doesn't think the train is a mistake. From what I hear, he's worked very hard to build the prototype.'

There was a knock on the door. Two waiters entered and set down trays of food on the table. For the next ten minutes there were no other sounds than the scraping of cutlery, requests for the passing of salt, and the slurping of drinks. Hal ate his dinner so fast, he barely chewed it.

'That's much better,' said Uncle Nat, once his plate was clean. He leaned back in his chair and patted his stomach. 'Now, let's go over the facts.' He held up his hand and counted off on his fingers. 'Somebody, a friend or a foe, sent August a beautiful gift but neglected to identify themselves. Francisco is worried about the test run tomorrow and wants it delayed because he fears the engine may fail. Also, he wishes people would acknowledge his work more than they do. There's a news crew who are hoping for a juicy story.' He looked at Marianne. 'Have I missed anything?'

'The mysterious man who delivered the parcel,' she reminded him.

'Ah, yes, the hotel says no such man exists and that they know nothing of a package for August.' Uncle Nat put up another finger. He paused, staring at his fingers for a moment. 'I can see why you're concerned, Marianne, but I don't think these things add up to a threat. What is it you're most worried about?'

'Boaz designed the Solar Express for a really good reason, and Pop is very proud of it,' Marianne said. 'I don't want anyone to spoil the day tomorrow.'

'Right, well, there are three of us.' Uncle Nat looked from her to Hal. 'We'll all be watching to make sure that nothing goes wrong tomorrow. Agreed?'

'Agreed,' they echoed.

There came another knock at the door, and to everyone's surprise a woman in a tight, silver tube dress tottered in on high heels. She had glossy black hair pinned up on top of her head, wore dangly gold earrings, and was strikingly pretty. 'G'd evening.' She smiled brightly. 'I'm Michelle.' She looked at Marianne. 'Your father sent me up to . . . ah, look after you.'

Uncle Nat got up. 'I'm Nathaniel Bradshaw.'

'Yes, hello, Mr Bradshaw. Mr Reza sends his apologies. He's only just now got back to the hotel and has a dinner he must attend. He sent me up to relieve you from having to look after his daughter. He sends his thanks and looks forward to seeing you tomorrow at the launch.'

'Pop sent you to babysit me?' Marianne sounded unimpressed. 'I'm thirteen!'

'You are a babysitter?' Uncle Nat asked, surprised.

'Good grief, no!' Michelle pulled a face. 'I'm Head of Communications for Reza Tech in Australia. I thought I was going to a fancy dinner tonight. Hence the outfit.' She did an awkward little curtsy. 'But Mr Reza needed someone to look after his daughter, and so . . . here I am.'

'Ah, well, we have a little problem. You see, Hal – that's my nephew – and Marianne were about to have a swim, but I won't let them go in the water until they've digested their food, and we've only just eaten.' He looked pointedly at the table covered in dirty dishes, then glanced at the three wrist watches he wore on his left arm, studying one thoughtfully. 'We probably won't be done for at least an hour and a half, possibly two.' He looked apologetic. 'I wonder, would you mind if I stayed? Hal really wants to swim – doesn't he, Marianne? And if I'm here, there's no need for you to be.'

It took Michelle a moment to realize Uncle Nat was telling her that she could go to her fancy dinner. 'Oh! Not at all, Mr Bradshaw.' She turned to Marianne, who was nodding and grinning. 'I'll let Mr Reza know that I'm not needed here.' She beamed. 'Thank you.'

She paused on her way out. 'I've gotta ask, why the three watches?'

'Six actually,' said Uncle Nat. He drew up his right sleeve, revealing three more. They tell me the time in London, Berlin, New York, Moscow, Tokyo and here.' He smiled. 'I travel a lot.'

'Cool!' Michelle replied, looking baffled and closed the door behind her.

'I wish people would stop making up stories about how desperate I am to swim!' Hal said and Marianne laughed.

'How long do we have to wait before we can get in the pool, Uncle Nat?' Hal asked.

'Oh, that digesting thing is a bit of made-up nonsense,' Uncle Nat admitted. 'You can jump in the water right now if you want to.'

They didn't need to be told twice. Within a minute, Hal and Marianne were in their swimsuits and leaping into the water.

CHAPTER SEVEN

THE PRESTIGE

At nine o'clock the next morning, Hal and Uncle Nat arrived at the door of the conference room, to be greeted by Michelle. Today her hair was sculpted into a neat bob and she was wearing a smart dress with a block pattern print of black, yellow and blue.

'Good morning, Nathaniel, Hal.' Her smile was professional. 'All passengers have reserved seats in rows three and four.' She crossed them off the list on her clipboard. 'Help yourself to a drink and a pastry.' She held out a hand to show them the way to the refreshment table, then looked over Uncle Nat's shoulder, shining her dazzling smile on the next person in line.

'Excellent,' Uncle Nat said, as they headed to the table. 'More coffee.'

Most of the people milling about were wearing lanyards around their necks with *PRESS* written on them. He supposed that everybody staying in the hotel had something to do with the day's event. 'Look, there it is, on the stage.' Hal nodded towards the model of the Rocket.

'Ah yes, the mystery gift.' Uncle Nat filled a cup from the coffee pot. 'Let's take a closer look.'

As they made their way to the front of the room, Hal spotted Tom Flinch, dressed in a smart blue suit and tie, standing beside Kira's camera. She was leaning against the wall, looking at her phone, while he anxiously surveyed the room. Hal had expected the news reporter would look smug after getting his interview with Francisco, and he wondered if it hadn't gone as planned. 'Marianne's not here yet. Neither is Boaz.'

'They'll be arriving soon,' Uncle Nat replied as they approached the stage. He leaned forward to examine the model. No one stopped him or told him off, and, not for the first time, Hal thought how much easier it would be to investigate things if he was a grown-up.

'Hal!' Uncle Nat whispered excitedly. 'Look at this mechanism, attaching the piston to the wheel. That is a functioning crankshaft.' He looked at Hal with delight. 'Your powers of observation are exceptional. Look, the wheels *are* lifted – what, two, maybe three millimetres above the tracks so they can turn around? Exactly like your sketch.' He leaned back to admire the miniature locomotive. 'How utterly extraordinary! Do you see how the piston is sectioned so you can see the workings of the machine? I have to admit, I wouldn't mind if someone gave this to me as a gift. It must be worth a small fortune!'

'Which makes it even stranger that the card wasn't signed,' Hal pointed out.

'August has many admirers. Whoever sent this wanted to get his attention. I wonder if the gift-giver wanted to reveal themselves in person, so that August might be more favourably disposed to agree to whatever it is that they want?'

'Do you mean the model could be a bribe?'

'If you gave me this, I'd let you have anything you wanted,' Uncle Nat replied. 'Now, I wonder where the operating switch is?' His fingers twitched, and Hal could see he was thinking about picking it up.

'*Ladies and gentleman, please can I have your attention.*' Uncle Nat and Hal both jumped guiltily as Michelle's peppy voice came through the speakers. '*If you'd like to take your seats, we'll begin.*'

Withdrawing from the stage, Hal and Nat went to sit down.

'Hey, look, it's that couple from The Ghan,' Hal said, seeing Karleen and Kenny at the refreshment table. They were both dressed in long shorts and colourful T-shirts, and Karleen had on a cheerful headscarf. 'I wonder why they're here,' he added, watching Kenny pouring coffee while Karleen loaded up her handbag with pastries. 'They look like they've wandered into the wrong room.'

'Let's sit there.' Uncle Nat pointed to the only two adjacent empty seats in a reserved row.

Shuffling along the aisle, Hal found himself sitting down beside an imposing woman who was taller than Uncle Nat. She was fair-skinned, with a platinum-blonde crop, and wearing a bottle-green trouser suit. Beyond her sat an athletic man, dressed in a charcoal suit. He had short black hair, styled with a quiff, and a sceptical expression.

'Ms Deane,' Uncle Nat leaned forward. 'It's a pleasure to make your acquaintance. I'm Nathaniel Bradshaw, and this is my nephew, Harrison. We are friends of August's and travelling on the Solar Express today.'

'Nice to meet you, Mr Bradshaw,' Leslie Deane replied. She gestured to the man beside her. 'This is Terry Chang. We're looking forward to seeing what August Reza's got in store for us today. He sure did talk big at dinner last night.'

Mr Chang nodded in greeting and then agreement with Leslie Deane.

'Hal!' Marianne called from across the room and waved. She was stood beside Kira's camera. He grinned, feeling a thrill of excitement.

'Showtime,' Uncle Nat said, under his breath.

The room was crackling with anticipation.

Michelle stepped on to the stage holding a microphone. 'Good morning, everyone. For those of you who don't know me, my name is Michelle Abbott. and I'll be taking care of you today. On behalf of Reza Technologies, I'd like to welcome you to an historic occasion. On this auspicious day, the world will witness – and some of you will take – the first ever journey of the Solar Express: *a train for our future.*' She paused for applause. 'At the end of this press conference, electric minibuses will transport you to Alice Springs station where the Solar Express awaits.' There were excited murmurs in the audience. 'But first, please, everybody put your hands together as I welcome to the stage August Reza . . .'

Appearing from behind a curtain, accompanied by a burst of music and tumultuous applause, August stepped up and walked to the middle of the stage. He paused, smiling as people clapped, then took the central seat at the table.

'. . . Francisco Silva,' Michelle continued, and there was another burst of music and applause, but this time no one appeared from behind the curtain. A blonde girl rushed over to Michelle and whispered something to her. 'My apologies,' Michelle said. 'I have made a mistake. Mr Silva is already at the station, making sure the Solar Express is ready for her first journey with passengers.'

The room rippled with a tide of whispers. Hal looked at the third empty chair and wondered if Mr Silva had done his interview with Tom Flinch that morning.

'But now is the moment I know you've all been waiting for,' Michelle went on, trying to get back the audience's attention. 'Please put your hands together and welcome to the stage . . . Mr Boaz Tudawali, inventor of the Solar Express.'

There was another stab of music as Boaz appeared. A blaze of camera flashes went off, accompanied by raucous applause and a wolf-whistle. Sitting down next to August, Boaz leaned forward to the microphone. 'Stop it, Ma,' he said, squinting against the flashes. 'I told you, there'll be plenty of time for pictures later.'

'Friends,' August said, as the laughter and applause died away. 'Today is the day. Today we celebrate the possibility of a future where no fossil fuels are burned. Where the challenge of the climate crisis is met.' There was a cheer. 'Where networks of clean, efficient, fast and affordable railways connect communities and create jobs.' Hal noticed Leslie Deane lean forward in her seat. August held up his hand. 'As with many of the solutions for the problems our planet faces, of the hundreds of applicants who entered the Reza's Rocket competition, the most inspiring ideas came from young people. As soon as I saw the design for the Solar Express, I knew we had the solution we've all been craving, and it came out of the mind of this young man beside me: Boaz Tudawali.'

'Hi.' Boaz waved, and there was an awkward pause. 'Oh, you're expecting a speech?' He grinned. 'I haven't written anything down. You see, I think it's pretty simple. There's power in the air we breathe, the light by which we see, and the water that we drink. My regenerative hydrogen fuel cell offers

us a way to generate power for a train, or any other vehicle, cleanly. There's no need for batteries. All we need is air, water, and sunlight. Here in Australia, we've got lots of all three.'

'We don't have much water,' came the sarcastic muttering of a journalist in the front row.

'You're wrong there, mate,' Boaz replied. 'We don't have much rain, but beneath the earth is the Great Artesian Basin. That's a huge lake three times the size of France. Back when the line to Alice used steam engines, they refuelled at pumping stations that bored straight down into it.'

'Bo-Bo clever!' came a young voice.

'Thanks, JJ.' Boaz waved. 'That's my little sister, everybody. Watch out for her. She bites.' The audience laughed warmly.

'At Reza Technologies,' August Reza said as the laughter subsided, 'my partner, Francisco Silva, has led a team of

chemists, computer scientists, and engineers, working with Mr Tudawali on his train's design. We hope that in the future, the Tudawali RFC will offer a completely clean alternative to *all* battery-powered electric vehicles, not just trains.' There was a murmur, and he lifted his chin to indicate that he hadn't finished talking. The room fell silent. 'I am announcing today a significant investment in the Northern Territory, where Reza Technologies are leasing land to build the world's largest solar farm. Energy from the solar farm and water from the Basin will be used to produce hydrogen on an industrial scale.' A couple of cameras clicked. 'We're here to tell you today that hydrogen is the clean energy of the future, and the Solar Express is a symbol of what is possible.'

The room burst into applause. People were on their feet.

Leslie Deane was standing too, but Hal noticed she wasn't clapping.

'Mr Reza,' a journalist called out. 'Mark Smith, *New York Times*. Isn't hydrogen a volatile gas? Could the Solar Express go the same way as the *Hindenburg*?'

'Does a train look like a giant bag of gas, floating in the sky, to you, Mr Mark Smith of the *New York Times*?' Boaz replied, laughing. 'You don't need to worry. Hydrogen is safer than gasoline, and hydrogen tanks are rigorously tested. They don't leak.'

Voices called out a barrage of questions as Michelle appeared with her arms up to show that the conference was ending. August and Boaz waved and left the stage.

'Hal,' Marianne called, crossing the room to talk to

him. 'I asked Pop. He said I could go in the bus with you.' She indicated with her thumb, pointing over her shoulder. 'Although Woody's got to come too.'

Woody waved but didn't smile.

'Uncle Nat thinks the mechanisms on the Rocket model work. He says there must be a switch that turns it on.' They turned to look at the model in its glass case, still on the stage.

'Oh dear!' Marianne said loudly. 'Pop's forgotten his model train. I'll bring it for him.' No one stopped her as she marched up to the stage and lifted it down, returning to them with her eyes shining. 'Let's open it and see.'

'Hal, we should head out to the lobby and wait for the bus,' Uncle Nat said, turning away from Leslie Deane. He smiled when he saw what Marianne had in her arms. 'Although, perhaps we should get, er, a bottle of water from the bar, first?' Uncle Nat gave Hal and Marianne a conspiratorial look and they all nodded at once.

'Woody, could you get us a couple of bottles of water please?' Marianne asked, putting the model down on the nearest table. Woody hesitated. 'I'll be safe. Mr Bradshaw's here and you'll be able to see me from the bar.'

Woody nodded and lumbered away.

Uncle Nat leaned over the model. 'See where the bottom of the glass meets the wood. There's sealant or fluid holding the case together. I wonder . . .' Checking his jacket pockets, he pulled out a thin leather wallet.

'What's that?' Marianne asked.

'A gentleman's grooming kit,' Uncle Nat replied, opening

67

it, and sliding out a metal nail file. He inserted the tip between the glass and the wood of the model, and pushed it up, piercing the seal as he pulled at the case. There was noise, like gummed paper peeling off a wall, and a *thunk* as the glass case lifted off. 'Well, that was easy!' Uncle Nat said, and then stopped, because something odd had happened to his voice.

Hal and Marianne laughed.

'You sound like a cartoon character,' Hal said. 'Say something else.'

'I don't know why my voice has become squeaky,' Uncle Nat said. The first words of his sentence were pitched high, but by the end his voice was normal again.

'Oh no!' Marianne pointed at the Rocket. 'Look!' The shining silver metal of the engine's round boiler had tarnished, becoming black and dull. 'How did that happen?' She looked from Hal to Uncle Nat in panic. 'Pop will know we opened it! He's gonna be so mad.'

CHAPTER EIGHT

THE VANISHING

When they stepped off the minibus at Alice Springs station, Hal shielded his eyes from the glare of the morning sun and saw a small crowd gathered behind a cordon.

Woody was carrying the Rocket model. Uncle Nat had put the glass case back over it, and Marianne had insisted the bodyguard take it, saying it was too heavy. Hal wondered if she was planning to blame him for the strange discolouring of the locomotive.

When Reza's sleek black limousine arrived, people waved and held up their phones to take selfies with the billionaire. August and Boaz got out of the back to a raucous cheer.

'We should get Boaz to look at the Rocket model,' Uncle Nat said.

'Why?' Hal asked.

'It was odd that my voice went squeaky when I lifted off the case. There's only one thing I know that does that to a person's voice.'

'Helium!' Hal said, remembering a helium balloon he'd

messed around with at his friend Ben's birthday party.

'Yes. I'm wondering if the locomotive case was sealed to keep the helium inside. Perhaps releasing the helium is what made the locomotive change colour.'

'But how?' Hal asked.

'Goodness knows.' Uncle Nat shook his head. 'I'm not a scientist. I don't know enough about metals or gases to answer that question.'

'Boaz does.' Marianne nodded. 'But he's a bit busy launching his train.'

'It seems like a very particular thing to do,' Uncle Nat said. 'Create something that changes colour when it's exposed to air. I don't understand what reason a person would have for doing such a complicated thing. Unless . . .'

'Unless the reason isn't a nice one,' Marianne finished his sentence.

'Precisely.'

Hal recognized the look of concern on his uncle's face and his pulse quickened. He put his hand to his pocket, feeling the reassuring rectangular shape of his sketchbook. If someone was planning to mess with August Reza, then he was going to make sure they didn't get away with it.

All thoughts of detective work were swept from Hal's head as they arrived on the platform and he saw the Solar Express. Here, at last, was Boaz's train. It looked awesome.

The locomotive was boxy and scarlet with silver handles and pipes. The windows of the driver's cabin were high up, in the square nose, and a flag displaying the blue sun logo flew from its roof. Four shimmering silver carriages were lined up behind it, each with the crest of a blue sun emblazoned on the side. They had cyan-tinted windows and a curved roof of glistening black solar panels. At the back of the train was a rusty blue and yellow NR3 diesel-electric engine.

'Why's that old loco attached to the train?' Hal asked his uncle.

'This is a test run of a new prototype. I'd imagine the NR3 is there to rescue us if the Solar Express breaks down.'

'I thought Boaz's locomotive would look more futuristic,' Hal mused, 'like the carriages.'

'They have to be certain the prototype works before they worry about making it look pretty.'

Michelle clapped her hands together and everyone fell silent.

Kira had her camera on a shoulder mount and was filming the train.

August stepped on to the red carpet that led to the open door of the first carriage. 'It is with great pride that I – that we –' he gestured for Boaz to join him on the carpet – 'invite you to take the first ever ride on the Solar Express.'

Photographers took pictures and then Michelle passed a bottle of champagne to August that was attached to the locomotive by a red ribbon. August presented the bottle ceremoniously to Boaz, who lifted it high and said, 'Here's to healing some of the harm humans have done.' With the ribbon taut, he swung it hard against the body of the engine. It smashed and everyone cheered.

'Let's ride these rails,' August said. 'Cleanly!' He held out his arm to Boaz, and they boarded the train together.

Hal glanced at Marianne, to see if she minded, but her expression was unreadable.

'It's time for our guests to climb aboard,' Michelle said, going to stand beside the carriage door with her clipboard. 'The Solar Express is about to depart.'

Tom positioned himself beside her, using the opportunity to interview the passengers as they climbed aboard.

'Ms Deane, Minister for Transport, what are your first impressions of the Solar Express?' Tom asked, thrusting his microphone at the stony-faced woman.

'Reza Technologies offers great opportunities for today's Australians.' Leslie Deane forced a smile. 'This new train *could* pioneer a new wave of environmentally responsible transport, not just for us, but for the whole world. Let's just hope the technology works.'

'Good day, sir, what's your name?' Tom asked an elderly gentleman at the head of the queue, whom Hal recognized as the white-haired man he'd drawn yesterday in the lobby. Today he was dressed smartly in a baggy brown suit and leaning on a walking stick.

'Bobby Benson . . .'

'Did you hear that?' Uncle Nat asked, looking over his shoulder.

'What?' Hal followed his uncle's gaze along the empty platform.

'I thought I heard banging.' Uncle Nat's brow furrowed

as he looked around. 'It must have come from the crowd.' He shook his head a little. 'Come on, we'd better join the line. This is one train I refuse to miss.'

Hal and Nat were the last passengers to board the Solar Express, and Michelle took the opportunity to thank Uncle Nat for letting her attend last night's dinner. 'PR isn't really the job for me,' she confessed. 'I studied physics at university. I've got a master's degree in it. I was hoping to make a good impression.'

'Did it work?' Uncle Nat asked.

'Hope so.' Michelle held up crossed fingers.

They mounted the steps into a lounge car decorated in cyan and white, with pale wood furnishings. Shallow, semicircular tables with chairs were attached to one wall, while along the other was a long sofa seat. At either end of the carriage were two screens. Each showed a graphic featuring information about their journey, alternating with a camera feed of the view from the front of the train. The graphic was a map of Australia with Alice Springs clearly marked and an icon of a locomotive glowing beside it. A six-digit clock above the map showed the time in hours, minutes and seconds.

Sitting down in the nearest empty chair, Hal put his sketchbook on the table and pulled the lid off his pen. Everyone who was taking the trip on the Solar Express was in this carriage.

As his pen conjured the scene onto paper, he recorded Leslie Deane and Terrance Chang at the far end of the carriage, sitting together, talking furtively. Karleen and Kenny

Sparks were either side of Bobby Benson on the sofa. Tom was kneeling in front of them, holding up his microphone. Kira was standing to one side, pointing the camera at the old man.

'I'll be seventy-nine this year,' he was saying. 'I'm the longest-serving engine driver in Australia. Steam, diesel, electric – you name it, I can drive it. Twenty years I worked on The Ghan and I was driving freight before that. This railway line is the backbone of my life. I met my wife in the Darwin rail yards, God rest her soul. We raised our kids in Adelaide.' He paused, remembering. 'I've spent many happy days riding these rails. When my old bosses told me I'd been chosen to travel on the first ever journey of the train of the future –' he puffed out a breath – 'you could've blown me down with a feather.'

'What do you make of it so far, Mr Benson?' Tom asked him.

'We haven't moved yet.' Bobby Benson pointed his stick at the window. 'Ask me again when we get to Tennant Creek. To be honest, I always thought the trains of the future would be nuclear-powered, like the submarines.'

Marianne pushed Woody towards Hal. He was still carrying the Rocket model, and Hal saw that Marianne was trying to keep herself between the model and her father, so that he wouldn't see that it had tarnished.

Uncle Nat had collected a glass of champagne from the bar and came towards them as Woody set the model down on the next table. They all looked at Boaz, who was standing by the entrance to the next carriage, talking with his dad and August Reza. Vincent had hold of JJ's hand, but she was pulling away, trying to escape his custody.

'Where is Marlee?' Hal asked Marianne. 'Aren't Koen and Allira coming?'

'Boaz says his mum has to work today, and that Koen and Allira are looking after the farm.'

Michelle entered the carriage, making a beeline for August. She pulled him away from his conversation with the Tudawalis. She whispered something to August and he frowned.

'What do you mean, Francisco isn't here? Where is he?' Michelle shrugged and August looked at his watch. 'We'll have to delay departure.' He shook his head. 'Do the presentation for the guests now, before we leave.'

'Yes, Mr Reza.'

'And when that stubborn mule arrives, you tell him that I'm not impressed. Whether he likes it or not, this test run *is* happening today.'

Hal stared at his drawing, hoping they couldn't tell that he was listening in. Where was Francisco Silva? Why hadn't he been at the press conference this morning? If Tom Flinch's expression was anything to go by, he hadn't turned up to their in-depth interview either.

Marianne was pulling Boaz towards the table with the model on it. Hal was interested in hearing what Boaz had to say about it, so he closed his sketchbook and joined them.

JJ broke free from her father and dashed towards Kira, calling out, 'Me, me. Look at me.' She danced madly for the camera and Karleen laughed, clapping as JJ capered and spun. Tom tried to move her away, so that he could finish his interview with Bobby Benson, and got a kick to the shin for his efforts.

'She's much more interesting than my old railway stories.' Bobby Benson chuckled, leaning on his stick as he got to his feet. 'If you'll excuse me, I need to visit the men's room.'

'It blackened as soon as you took the case off?' Boaz was asking Uncle Nat.

'Yes. I must've breathed in because my voice went squeaky,' said Uncle Nat. 'We guessed it contained helium.'

'Hm.' Boaz lifted the glass case and sniffed the locomotive. 'Smell that?'

Marianne raised her eyebrows as Hal leaned forward and sniffed.

'It's like dirty nappies.' Hal wrinkled his nose.

'Ammonia,' said Boaz. He put the case back on. 'The blackened metal is probably lithium.' He scratched his head. 'But I don't get it. Why would you make the boiler out of lithium on a model like this? It doesn't make sense.'

'Could I have your attention, everyone,' Michelle said from the other end of the carriage. 'Before we set off, I would like to go through today's itinerary.' She held up a piece of paper. 'After departure, you will be able to finish your drinks while enjoying the spectacular landscape north of Alice Springs from here in the lounge, or from the observation pod, which you'll find on the other side of the dining car, through the doors behind me. Feel free to move about as you please and make yourselves comfortable. The fourth carriage contains your luggage and twelve coach-class seats, as an example of what a standard carriage might be like on a Reza train.' She drew breath. 'The journey to Tennant Creek is just over five hundred kilometres, and will take us approximately four and a half hours. The Solar Express will be travelling at a top speed of one hundred and twenty kilometres per hour.

'During our trip, I will be inviting you in small groups to visit the locomotive cabin where Boaz and Francisco will explain how this revolutionary engine works.' She glanced nervously at August. 'Then we will be eating a gourmet sushi lunch, in the dining car, created for you by August Reza's personal chef.' She looked about with an extra-dazzling smile to show what a treat this was. 'We arrive in Tennant Creek at about two thirty in the afternoon, where a minibus will take you to the airport. Reza Technologies has chartered a private plane to take you onwards to Darwin.' She smiled again, and Hal wondered if her cheeks ached. 'We have a film crew from World News on board the train, who are officially covering this story –' she gestured to Tom and Kira – 'so if you have enjoyed the experience, please do tell them.' She laughed. 'And of course, I am here to answer any questions you might have about the day.' She held up her hands. 'And that's it. Everybody, enjoy your drinks. We will be departing shortly.'

There was a polite patter of applause, and then the low hum of conversation resumed.

Hal watched Michelle go and have another whispered conversation with August, who left the train. Five minutes later, August returned looking annoyed. The door to the carriage beeped and closed behind him.

'Ladies and gentlemen,' Michelle cried, holding up a glass of champagne, 'I propose a toast to Boaz Tudawali's regenerative hydrogen fuel cell and the Solar Express.'

Everyone gave a loud cheer, especially JJ, and then the carriage was filled with the *ching* of glasses kissing. Hal looked at Boaz and grinned, feeling a thrill of delight as he heard a low hum, and the train rolled out of Alice Springs station. Turning to look out of the window, he saw the crowd behind the rope cordon waving madly, and he waved back, trying to ignore the sensation he had at the back of his mind that something wasn't right.

CHAPTER NINE

STRANGERS ON A TRAIN

'Before you venture off to explore,' Michelle said, holding up her hands, 'I thought it would be a good idea for us to introduce ourselves to each other. After all, we are going to be spending the next five hours together.' There was an uncomfortable silence and Hal was relieved to see that the adults in the carriage looked as unenthusiastic about this idea as he was. 'I'll go first, shall I? You all know that my name is Michelle Abbott, and that I'm Head of Communications for Reza Tech Australia, but what you don't know is that I'm a qualified physicist and one day I hope to join Mr Silva's team of engineers.'

She shot a look at August, but he wasn't listening. He was staring out the window, a troubled expression on his face.

'Who'd like to go next?' Michelle turned to her right, looking expectantly at Terrance Chang.

Mr Chang blinked, but then looked at the other passengers in the carriage and said, 'My name is Terry Chang. I'm

President of Chang Corp. I'm on the Solar Express because August would like me to believe that one day hydrogen might power my fleet of ships.' He gave a short staccato laugh, as if the idea were foolish.

At the sound of his name, August snapped out of his daze.

'For those of you who don't know me, I'm Leslie Deane.' The politician smiled. 'I'm here because I'm the Transport Minister for the Australian government.'

'We need the support of government,' Boaz said, 'to change things.'

'Yes, you will,' Leslie replied ambiguously, and Hal couldn't tell whether she meant to help or not.

Kenny took a sip from his glass of champagne, then smacked his lips. 'G'day, I'm Kenny Sparks and this is my beautiful wife, Karleen.'

'We're the competition winners,' Karleen said. 'We just love travelling.' She counted off on her fingers. 'We've been to Indonesia, America, England, China . . .'

'When we heard about the raffle to win tickets to travel on the Solar Express, we just had to enter,' Kenny said.

'And we won!' Karleen said, wearing a delighted expression as she threw up her hands.

'We got lucky.' Kenny grinned.

'Kenny's the luckiest man I've ever met,' Karleen gushed. 'He's always winning things.'

'I hit the jackpot when I met you.' Kenny winked at her.

'You charmer.' Karleen giggled and gave him a shove.

Hal liked Kenny and Karleen, but he could see that their

affection for one another bothered Leslie Deane; her nostrils flared with disgust as they teased one another.

'Shall I fill in for Bobby?' Karleen lowered her voice to a stage whisper. 'He's in the men's room.' She took the silence as a signal to continue. 'OK, sitting with us is a cutie called Bobby Benson. He's a retired train driver from Adelaide, and what he doesn't know about Australia's railways isn't worth knowing, I reckon.' She turned and looked at Tom. 'Your turn.'

'Um, my name's Tom Flinch, and I'm a journalist for World News.' He pushed his glasses up his nose. 'We were invited by Reza Tech to cover this trip and I'm hoping to interview all of you before we arrive in Tennant Creek.'

'Hi, I'm Kira Tate, camera operator for World News.' She dipped her head to show that this was all she would be saying.

'I'm Vincent. I'm Boaz's father.' He smiled at his son. 'I'm here with JJ, representing the Tudawalis. Boaz's ma can't be here. She's a pilot for the Royal Flying Doctor Service. She had to work today. But our whole family believes in what Boaz and Mr Reza are doing in creating this train, and we couldn't be prouder.'

'My name's JJ,' Boaz's sister said, then when everyone looked at her, she became shy and hid behind her father's leg.

Hal suddenly found everyone turning to look at him. His mind went blank. 'Err, I'm Harrison Beck . . .' *What should he say? That he solved crimes by drawing? That'd he'd met August Reza when his daughter had been kidnapped last year?* 'And I'm here because . . . I'm Marianne's friend. And I love trains.'

Marianne smiled at Hal, looking genuinely pleased. 'I'm Marianne Reza,' she said, then turning to the rest of the guests, 'and I'm here because my pop said that I had to come.' Karleen and Terry Chang chuckled. 'Oh, and this is Woody. He's my personal security. He doesn't talk much.'

Woody nodded.

'I'm Nathaniel Bradshaw.' Uncle Nat leaned forward. 'I'm a travel writer and Harrison's uncle.'

'Well, you know who I am,' Boaz said. 'Probably be sick of the sound of me by the end of today.'

'I doubt that very much,' August said, as the introductions came full circle. 'It's a pleasure to meet all of you.'

'Where's Francisco?' Terry glanced around the carriage. 'Is he at the front of the train?'

'Unfortunately, Francisco was unable to join us,' August said, 'but we'll be meeting up with him in Tennant Creek.' He smiled, but Hal could see he was tense. 'I hope you're all going to enjoy your journey. I know from experience that your lunch will be excellent, and I highly recommend spending time in our observation pod.' He moved to leave, and as he passed Boaz, he muttered, 'Could I have a word?'

Boaz and Michelle followed August out of the carriage.

'Wonder what happened to Francisco?' Terry said to Leslie. 'He and August exchanged some pretty strong words at dinner last night.'

'I don't know.' Leslie frowned. 'There's plenty of stories about those two having disagreements of opinion, but I don't think they've ever fallen out before.'

Terry lowered his voice. 'Do you think Francisco Silva is jealous of August Reza's new protégé?'

Leslie laughed quietly and nodded. 'It's never nice to be replaced by a younger model.'

'Do you want to go see the observation pod?' Karleen said, getting up and pulling Kenny to his feet. 'It sounds futuristic.'

'Excuse me, Ms Deane.' Tom was sidling nervously towards her. 'I wondered if we might ask you a few questions? I know our viewers would be interested in the opinions of Australia's next prime minister.'

Leslie's cool look warmed considerably. 'There's no way of knowing who will become the next prime minister.'

Kira was using a smaller, hand-held camera to film on the train, and already had it trained on the politician.

'According to the polls, you're the hot favourite to win.' Tom smiled winningly at Leslie. 'If you put yourself forward for the job, that is. Do you think you will?'

'Who knows?' Leslie shrugged, but the glint in her eye said that she would.

'And do you think you'll be supporting Reza Tech's application to lease land for clean hydrogen production?' Tom asked, as lightly as if he were asking what her favourite colour was.

Leslie seemed startled by this direct question. She smiled into the camera. 'Australia's fortunes were built on its mining industry. I wouldn't do anything to damage it. I'm proud to be Australian.'

Hal noticed a look of approval on Terry Chang's face.

'I think we should confess to your father that we opened the case of his model,' Uncle Nat was saying to Marianne.

'I don't know.' Marianne chewed nervously at her fingernail. 'Pop seems a bit stressed right now.'

'I'll take the blame,' Uncle Nat reassured her. 'It was me who opened it, after all.'

'Did you find the switch that makes the mechanism in the model work?' Hal asked.

The three of them leaned towards the model.

'Do you know, I was so taken aback when the boiler blackened, I forgot we were looking for a switch. I don't see anything obvious.'

'Do you think it could be the regulator?' Hal said, pointing to a tiny copper lever.

'What's the regulator?' Marianne asked, as he pushed the copper switch backwards and forwards. Nothing happened.

'It's the valve that releases compressed steam into the

pistons. Sometimes it's called the throttle.'

'Maybe the switch is on this wagon bit?' Marianne said.

'That's the tender,' Hal said. 'It's where they keep the coal for the firebox. And you see that barrel? That's where the water is kept, for the boiler.'

'It's got a tiny crack that goes all the way around it.' Marianne pointed. 'Do you think the barrel opens?' She pulled at it, but nothing moved.

'That's enough.' Uncle Nat blocked Hal and Marianne's prodding fingers with his hand. 'If we're not careful, we'll break it and then we'll really be in trouble.'

Boaz returned to the carriage. He looked directly at Hal, widening his eyes as he said, 'Who wants to be the first group to see around the driver's cabin? Get the guided tour?'

'Me!' Hal's hand shot up. 'Please can we go first, Uncle Nat?'

'Ah, yes.' Uncle Nat blinked. 'As long as that's OK with everyone?' He looked over at Tom and Kira, who nodded. 'We'll let you finish your interview in peace, shall we?' He got to his feet and picked up the Rocket model. 'Come on, Marianne, you're coming too. Yes, and you, Woody.'

'Follow me,' Boaz said. As he led them towards the locomotive, Hal moved to walk beside him.

'Is everything OK?'

'I don't know, mate.' Boaz shook his head. 'Something weird's going on.'

CHAPTER TEN

FIRESTARTER

A narrow corridor took them past the engine room to the driver's cabin. An angry August was striding backwards and forwards inside a room that made Hal think of the spaceships he'd seen in movies. The control desk had five screens, each with keypads beside them, and a lever that looked like a joystick beside a cluster of buttons. He thought the panoramic windows ought to show twinkling stars in an infinite universe, rather than rail tracks, on red earth, stretching to a blue horizon. According to a digital speedometer on the nearest screen, the locomotive was travelling at one hundred and fifteen kilometres an hour, and yet no one was sitting in the driver's seat. Hal leaned his sketchbook against the wall, to draw the console.

'Nathaniel.' August stopped pacing and stared in surprise at the Rocket model in his arms. 'What have you got that for? I thought I'd left it in the conference room to be packed away and sent to the head office back in Sydney.'

'I've got a confession to make,' Uncle Nat said. 'I fancied

that the mechanism worked, so I looked for a switch to turn it on . . .'

'I don't have time to worry about that right now.' August waved a hand at him. 'Listen, you heard that Francisco isn't on board?'

'Yes, you said—'

'Ignore what I said. I was lying. No one knows where he is. When he didn't turn up to the conference this morning, I assumed he'd be at the station.'

'Do you think he's at the hotel?'

'I called the hotel before we left Alice Springs. He's not in his room. No one has seen him since breakfast, at seven o'clock this morning.' August slapped the back of his hand against the wall in

frustration. 'Of all the times to pull a disappearing trick.'

'How can we help?' Uncle Nat asked calmly, handing the Rocket model to Hal.

Hal glanced at Marianne. He'd never seen August angry before.

'Francisco was supposed to be giving our guests a guided tour of the technology we're using.' He waved at the driving controls.

'I can tell people about how the fuel cell works and supplies the engine with power,' Boaz said, 'but the technology driving the train was designed by his team.'

'Driverless trains aren't new,' August said. 'Many city metro systems are driverless, and the mining industry here uses driverless freight

trains, but Francisco's team have developed a self-driving system that uses satellites to spy miles up the track to respond to any kind of obstacle or possible situation in plenty of time. It's much safer than having a driver. Problem is, I have no idea how it works.'

Hal stared at the empty chair behind the console. It was eerie watching the train gobble up track without anyone being at the controls. 'If you don't need a driver, then why's there a desk with a seat?'

'Technology can sometimes have . . . glitches,' August replied. 'The control desk has a manual override as a safety precaution. We don't anticipate it ever being used.' He slipped his hand under his glasses and rubbed his eyes. 'My big problem is Leslie Deane, Terry Chang and those idiots from World News.'

'Why?' Hal asked.

'There's a lot riding on this test run,' replied August. 'We need Leslie Deane on our side, because we've made a crucial application to lease land for a hydrogen production facility and a factory to make the Tudawali RFC. It's with the Australian government right now. Without Leslie's help the whole project could fail. Terry has expressed an interest in adapting the Tudawali RFC for his shipping fleet, which could be a big deal, but I suspect he's really here to check out the competition.' He looked out the window. 'Francisco not showing up makes us seem chaotic and unreliable.'

'Why do you think he didn't turn up at the conference this morning?' Uncle Nat asked.

'Francisco gets nervous talking to audiences. He's not a public speaker. I couldn't tell you the number of times he's not shown up to these things. It didn't surprise me at all.'

'It surprised me,' Boaz said. 'He promised me he'd be there to answer any tricky questions.'

'That *is* out of character,' August agreed. 'I didn't think he would let Boaz down.'

'Did you know he'd agreed to do an interview with World News before the conference this morning?' Hal asked.

'No.' August looked surprised.

'I could ask Tom Flinch if he turned up.'

'I don't think that's a good idea. I can't have World News reporting that Reza Tech has lost its Chief Technical Officer. I need them to tell the world that the test ride is a big success. There are a lot of potential investors watching.' He sighed. 'You'd be surprised how much of business is putting on a show.'

'People know you two were arguing at dinner last night, Pop,' Marianne said.

'Francisco and I are like brothers. We fight all the time. It doesn't mean anything.'

'Francisco wanted you to postpone today's launch, didn't he?' Hal asked.

'He said the locomotive wasn't ready yet, and that if it failed it would be his team that looked bad, that it was his reputation on the line. But he's always worried that things aren't ready. Technology is iterative, you've got to try things and fail to find out what needs improvement.' He gestured to the windscreen. 'And look. The train is working perfectly.'

'So, what are you going to do?' Uncle Nat asked.

'I don't know! I don't program software or manage technical builds. I do the big picture stuff: the design, the experience, the messaging.' He looked rattled. 'I could say that Francisco was taken ill.' He looked at Boaz. 'Boaz and I are going to have to give a presentation to Leslie, Terry and the news crew.'

'I can talk about the fuel cell and try and fill in for Francisco,' Boaz offered. 'I know a bit.'

'I know who you should get to help you,' Marianne said. 'Michelle. She wants to work on Francisco's team. She was at the dinner last night. I'll bet she talked to him about –' she waved her hand at the control panel – 'how this works.'

'Yes!' Hal agreed with Marianne. 'Michelle's a physicist.'

August stared at his daughter. 'That's a good idea.'

'I know.' Marianne smiled cheerily.

'Thank you.'

'Any time. I'm just glad you aren't mad that we broke your Rocket model.'

'You *broke* it?'

'I was trying to tell you.' Uncle Nat stepped forward. 'It's my fault. I thought there might be a switch inside the case that worked the mechanism of the model. As you can see, those sectioned cylinders have pistons inside that are connected to the wheels.' August's eyebrows lifted. 'I broke the seal as I opened the case. It was filled with helium gas. When the Rocket model was exposed to air it blackened and tarnished.'

'I think the boiler is made of lithium,' Boaz said. 'Lithium is a shiny silver, but it goes black when it reacts with the nitrogen in the air and smells of nappies.'

August lifted off the glass case, and leaned in to examine his model. 'So it has.'

'We think the model works, Pop.' Marianne moved to stand beside him.

'I thought the regulator might be the on switch,' Hal said.

August pushed the tiny lever.

With the model right under his nose, Hal's nostrils caught a whiff of something familiar. 'Can anyone smell gas?'

Uncle Nat leaned over and sniffed. 'A trace.' He studied the footplate of the Rocket. 'The Rocket was invented before brakes. The only controls were the regulator, a handbrake to clamp the wheel once the locomotive was stationary, and this pedal here.' He pointed. 'The reversing pedal. Because the Rocket had no brakes, if you wanted to stop, you'd stamp on it, and it would channel steam to the piston that turns the wheels backwards. The loco would come to a stop, before reversing.' He pushed down the tiny reversing pedal and an ignition spark flared inside the model firebox, triggering a crackle of scarlet fire, and suddenly the entire boiler was engulfed in red flames.

'Argh!' Hal jumped back, letting go of the model.

Boaz, who'd been standing beside him, dropped down, catching the wooden base before it hit the floor. He held it at arm's length. The boiler was burning vigorously, spitting crimson sparks.

'Isn't that hurting you?' Marianne cried, as Boaz scanned the cabin.

'Nah, got asbestos hands thanks to years of playing with fire.' He looked at Hal. 'Mate, I'm going to need you to grab that fire blanket hanging on the wall behind you. If anyone can see a fire extinguisher, we could use it right now. Lithium fires are deadly hard to put out.'

Woody dashed into the corridor.

Hal yanked the fire blanket from its container. 'What now?' he asked, feeling the heat of the fire on his face.

'Lay it on the floor.'

Boaz was carefully lowering the flaming model to the floor when there was a *click*. The locomotive and tender tumbled off the tracks and crashed on to the blanket. Boaz swore under his breath, tossing the wooden base aside. Woody appeared with a fire extinguisher. Boaz grabbed it, pulling the trigger and unloading a torrent of powder at the engine. After he'd emptied it, he dived forwards and wrapped the blanket over it.

'We should submerge the whole

thing in water,' Boaz said, 'once the fire is extinguished and the lithium's all used up.'

'There's a bathroom this way,' said Woody.

Boaz scooped up the blanket and followed him

'Who sent this to you?' Uncle Nat asked August.

'I don't know,' August whispered. 'I thought . . . I thought it was sent by a supporter, to curry favour.' He looked shocked.

Hal and Marianne exchanged a worried glance.

'I've got a bad feeling about this,' Hal said.

CHAPTER ELEVEN

CLIFFHANGER

'You must see that model for what it is,' Uncle Nat said to August. 'It's an attack on you.'

'It might not be,' Marianne said. 'I know it went on fire and everything, but no one could have known that we'd take the glass case off, turn the lever and press the pedal thing. There are better ways to attack a person.'

'It's a message,' Hal said. 'When we started the engine, it burst into flames and derailed.'

There was an uncomfortable silence.

'It could just be a faulty gift,' August said, but his words were hollow. Hal could tell that he didn't believe them.

'All taken care of,' said Boaz, returning with Woody. 'Although no one is to use the driver's bathroom. The model is underwater, in the sink. It needs to stay there till we get to Tennant Creek. If we pull it out, the lithium could reignite.'

'Woody, I think we need to assume someone wishes August harm,' Uncle Nat said.

'Now, wait a minute, let's not get carried away,' August

protested. 'I get threatened, er –' he glanced at Marianne – 'sometimes, and it's nearly always empty words sent to disrupt a project or prevent me from doing what I need to do. If I pay attention to every threat I get, I'd never leave the house.'

'Yes, but this isn't just words.' Uncle Nat picked up the scorched wooden base from the floor. 'Someone went to an awful lot of trouble to make that model.'

'What would you have me do?' August looked from Uncle Nat to Woody. 'Stop the train? Turf everyone off into the Outback and say, "Sorry, some crazy person sent me a model train, so we'll have to reschedule"? I can't do that. You know I can't do that. I *won't* do that.'

There was a long silence.

'Every passenger on this train has had a thorough background check. My people know everything about them, their family, and their family's family.' He paused to let his words sink in. 'Francisco was worried the fuel cells wouldn't produce enough power to pull the Solar Express out of the station, but the train is performing well.' He pointed. 'That blasted model is supposed to be back at the hotel. If you hadn't brought it here, we wouldn't be having this conversation.' The pitch of his voice was rising. 'I don't need extra problems right now. I'm still trying to deal with the fact that Francisco decided not to show up to work today.' He folded his arms. 'So, let's get Michelle in here, and get on with it.'

'I'll find her,' Marianne volunteered, slipping out.

'August,' Uncle Nat said quietly, 'if that model is a message, it would be a good idea to run a check on the train's systems. Make sure everything is behaving as it should. Is that possible?'

'It *is* possible.' August sighed. 'However, only Francisco, or a member of his team, knows how to do it.'

'What about calling someone?' Hal suggested, trying to helpful. 'Could they guide you through it, or Boaz?'

'We're in the Outback,' Boaz said. 'There's no mobile signal. No wi-fi neither.'

'Look, I may not know how to perform a systems check,' August said, 'but if I need to, I know how to turn off the computer and apply the brake.'

Uncle Nat stared flatly into August's eyes.

'You *can't* be suggesting that I stop the train? The news networks would have a field day. What kind of message would that send about the Solar Express? No. I'm not playing into the whole Hindenburg effect.' August shook his head. 'This is ridiculous. You're letting your imagination run away with itself. That model means nothing. I'm not stopping this train because of that.'

'Sir,' Hal said quietly. 'Couldn't you say that, as part of the test run, Boaz is going to perform some routine checks? Or that you thought stopping the train for lunch would be nice?' He stepped towards August. 'Your daughter is on this train. Wouldn't it be better to make sure it's safe? Then we can continue the journey and really enjoy it.'

'My little sister's on board,' Boaz added.

August Reza dropped his head into his hands. 'Urgh, OK,' he groaned.

'You needed me?' came Michelle's perky voice, as she and Marianne appeared in the doorway of the crowded cabin.

'Ah, Michelle, yes, good.' Uncle Nat turned at her. 'August is going to stop the train.'

'He is?' Michelle looked at August in surprise.

'Yes, Michelle, I need your help. I want the passengers to think the Solar Express stopping was always on today's schedule, and that there's nothing to worry about. If anyone asks, we'll say that Boaz is performing efficiency tests on the fuel cells.'

'Got it,' she replied. 'Is there something to worry about?'

'Nope.' August shook his head and forced a smile. 'Everything is going to plan. It's just that, without Francisco, things are a bit more complicated than we'd like.'

'Right.' Michelle looked around the cabin at everyone's serious faces. 'I think I understand.'

'I can't believe I'm doing this,' August muttered as he sat down in the driver's seat in front of the controls. 'This switch overrides the autopilot and activates the desk,' he muttered, reminding himself how it worked as he pushed the switch up. 'And this lever is the brake.' He pulled a T-shaped lever slowly towards him. The noise of the engine didn't change.

August frowned, looking down at the lever. He glanced at Boaz. 'This is the brake, isn't it?'

Boaz nodded slowly and the colour drained from August's face.

Hal's stomach dropped into his shoes. According to the digital speedometer, they were still travelling at one hundred and fifteen kilometres an hour. The train hadn't slowed down at all.

Sitting bolt upright, August flicked open a clear plastic cover protecting a round red button and slammed his fist down on it.

Nothing happened.

Boaz dropped on to his knees, swiftly rolling on to his back, and sliding under the console. He reached up, yanking down a ball of wires that fed into a circuit board. He studied it, making a sound like someone had punched him in the stomach. He held out a red wire so that they could see it had been severed.

'Someone's been under here with a knife,' he said. 'The Solar Express has been sabotaged.'

CHAPTER TWELVE

UNSTOPPABLE

Hal stared at the cut wire in Boaz's hands. He could hear the sound of the wheels rolling over train tracks. No one spoke for the longest time.

Someone doesn't want the Solar Express to be stopped. But why?

Reaching out, August lifted a telephone handset connected to the desk. He pressed a button. 'Hello? August Reza here. Hello? *Hello?*' He waited, then put the receiver down. Drawing in a long slow breath, he turned to face them. Speaking in a remarkably calm voice, he said, 'Firstly, let me reassure you all that there is no need for panic.' His voice was measured and confident, but there was a sheen of sweat on his forehead. 'There are a number of ways we can solve this problem.'

'Good.' Uncle Nat seemed to have grown taller and older. 'What are they?'

Everyone in the cabin was on edge.

August helped Boaz to his feet, buying himself some

thinking time. 'First, we must find out what our saboteur hopes to achieve.' He pointed to the console. 'Despite cut wires, the computer is still successfully driving this train.' He gave them a nervous smile.

Hal did not find August's words reassuring.

'Do we *know* it's the Reza Tech computer program that's driving the Solar Express?' Uncle Nat asked.

'That is a good question,' August agreed.

'Whoever made that Rocket model was very clever,' Hal said. 'It was thought through step by step. What has cutting those wires done?'

August looked at Boaz.

'They've destroyed the manual override and the emergency brake,' Boaz said. 'Possibly done more damage. I don't know how much of the console is working.'

'The computer can still drive us all safely to Tennant Creek,' August said.

'But,' Michelle said softly, 'if they loaded a new program into the computer and *then* cut the wires . . . someone else could be controlling this train.'

They stared at the bank of computer screens.

'How would someone load a new program into the train's computer?' Uncle Nat asked.

'Those ports.' August pointed to two slits in the surface of the desk. He pulled a black and orange plastic card from his pocket. 'These are Reza Tech memory keys. They go in those slots. They verify who you are and your level of access. They can also carry data. Only someone with one of these, with a new program already on it, could access the train's hard drive and change its driving instructions.'

'Is it possible to alter the software remotely?' Uncle Nat asked. 'From your office, while the train is motion?'

'One day, perhaps,' August replied. 'But, as I said, there's no wi-fi or mobile signal in the Outback. We're using the Reza Tech satellite system to communicate with the train.' He pointed at the phone. 'I should be able to talk with the train tech team using that, but it's dead.'

'Does that mean the satellite feed has been cut?' Uncle Nat said.

August nodded. 'Without the satellite link-up, the tech team can't communicate with the train's computer. We're alone out here.'

'How many people have one of those cards?' Hal asked, pointing.

'Right now, in Australia, only three people. Me, Francisco, and the head engineer on this project, Jed. He's with the team in Tennant Creek.'

'Could Jed have come to Alice Springs yesterday?' Uncle Nat asked.

'No. I spoke to him this morning.'

'If there's one card in Tennant Creek,' Hal said, 'and you have one . . .'

'Francisco!' Marianne gasped.

'No,' August shook his head. 'Francisco wouldn't . . .'

'Then where is he?' Uncle Nat asked quietly.

'Um . . .' Michelle raised her hand. 'Could I take a look

at the monitors? I'm not an expert on driving trains, but my undergrad degree was a BSc in computer science and physics, and my MSc is in computational physics. I might be able to help.'

Looking at Michelle as if he'd only just met her, August handed her his key card. 'Be my guest.'

'Do you have a password?' Michelle asked, sitting down in the driver's chair.

August leaned down and whispered something in her ear.

'Oh Mr Reza, that's not a very safe password. I would've guessed that on my second or third try.' She shook her head. 'When we get back to the office, you should change it.'

August straightened up, looking chastened.

Michelle tucked her hair behind her ears, then slotted the key card into the dashboard. The password entry screen flashed up on the left-hand screen. There was a strip of number keys beside the screen that were still working. She typed in August's password, hitting return.

ACCESS DENIED, the screen read.

'What?' August leaned forward. 'That's not right. Try it again.' Michelle removed the key card, reinserted it and typed the password in again.

ACCESS DENIED.

'That's the first thing I would do too,' Michelle said. 'I mean, if I was hijacking this train – which I'm not, obviously.' She laughed nervously. 'What I mean is –' she looked at August – 'when you find out your train has been sabotaged, the first thing you're gonna do is hit the emergency brake –

which you did – and when that didn't work, you'd try the phone.' She pointed. 'And then you'd log into the journey software and try to rewrite it so that the train stops. That's why they've scrambled the passwords, so you can't log in.'

'Wait.' Hal held up his pen, pausing his sketch. 'Whoever did this made assumptions about what we'd do when. But no one could have known that we'd bring the Rocket model on to the train, work out it was some kind of threat, and attempt to stop the train *now*.' He looked around at their concerned faces. 'We're *early*. The saboteur can't know that we've discovered what they've done to the train!'

'Yes!' August said, a glimmer of hope igniting in his eyes.

'Right now, the Solar Express is travelling as it should be. The train tech team in Tennant Creek will think the journey is going as planned. I would've thought that everything was going smoothly too, if you hadn't brought that blasted exploding engine in here.'

'We've got a head start on the dingo,' Boaz said. 'We can work out what they're up to and put a stop to it.'

'But we don't know how much of a head start we've got,' Hal said.

'I could try and hack into the computer system,' Michelle suggested.

'You're a hacker?' August looked shocked.

'It's just a hobby,' Michelle muttered. 'I've never managed to crack any of Francisco's security encryptions.'

'But you've tried?' August pressed, and Michelle's face went bright pink. She stuttered something inaudible about idle hours at university.

'I doubt I'll be able to rewrite the program, but I might be able to see what the new one is going to make the train do.' Michelle slid off the chair on to her knees and pulled at the fibreglass panel at the back of the console desk. Boaz got down beside her and helped yank it free. Behind it was a tangle of wires, circuit boards and metal boxes.

'What am I going to tell the passengers?' August muttered, pulling at his bottom lip with his thumb and forefinger.

'I think it's best that you don't tell them anything,' Uncle Nat replied. 'At least, not yet. If the saboteur's plan is to destroy the Solar Express project before it's had a chance to get investment and public backing, then we don't want to play into their hands.'

'We can't tell the other passengers,' Hal agreed. 'One of them could be the saboteur. If we tell them, we may lose our head start.' He flicked back to the picture he'd drawn of all the guests in the lounge, studying them.

There was an uncomfortable silence as everyone thought about the other passengers, wondering if the saboteur was on the train.

'Yes. We must keep this a secret from everyone else,' August said, sounding relieved. 'Including your father, Boaz.'

Boaz didn't look happy about this, but he nodded.

'We've only got a small window of time to work out what the saboteur is planning,' Hal said. 'Let's get to work.'

CHAPTER THIRTEEN

TOTAL RECALL

'How long have we been in the driver's cabin?' Marianne asked. 'It'll look suspicious if we're in here too long.'

'Yes,' Hal agreed. 'I'm going to explore the train and find somewhere to draw and think.'

'I'll come with you,' Uncle Nat said.

'Me too.' Marianne linked her arm through her bodyguard's. 'Come on, Woody. I want you to follow me now.'

'Boaz, Michelle and I will work on the train's computer,' August said. 'We've got a bit of time before we have to invite the next group in for the talk.'

'You're still going to give them a tour of the driver's cabin?' Uncle Nat was surprised.

'It's best to continue as normal.' August nodded. 'If one of the passengers is the saboteur, they might give themselves away. We'll be on the lookout for any odd questions or behaviour.'

'Good idea,' Hal said.

'We should go.' Marianne went to the door.

As they passed through the lounge, into the dining car, Hal studied Leslie and Terry, who were still being interviewed by Tom and Kira. *Could one of them be the saboteur?*

In the dining car, they found Vincent trying to stop JJ from grabbing food from a silver trolley, set up for the lunch service.

'No, JJ. That's not for you. I've got snacks in my bag. Come away.'

'I need wee-wee,' JJ replied, dancing about.

The observation pod was a giant white chrysalis with an asymmetrical mosaic of unusually shaped windows stretching from the floor to the apex of the roof. A long double-sided seat snaked down the middle of the carriage, so people could sit back-to-back admiring the view. At night, they could lie down and look up through the roof at the star-speckled sky. The dazzling whiteness of the carriage made the vermilion earth and cobalt sky outside seem even more vivid. The deeper into Australia he travelled, the redder the earth seemed to get. Hal understood why this part of the great continent Oceania was named the Red Centre.

'What a wonderful room to see the world from,' Uncle Nat said. 'It feels like an art gallery.'

The low, rhythmic vibrations of a didjeridu played through hidden speakers. Hal heard a second didjeridu, higher pitched than the first, making animal-like calls. A shaker and a chiming bell punctuated the rhythm of the mesmerizing music. Hal found himself calming down. 'I like it in here,' he said, taking a seat. 'It's a good place to draw.'

'Isn't it cool?' Marianne sat down beside him. 'I saw the designs but it's much better in real life.'

Woody stood beside the door. Uncle Nat talked politely to him, though the bodyguard only ever nodded or shook his head and never took his eyes off Marianne.

'Talk about disappointing,' Karleen's voice said, as the door at the far end of the pod opened and she, Kenny and Bobby came through it. 'A pile of suitcases, a bathroom and some seats! After this carriage, I was expecting a portal to another dimension!'

'Oh, I don't know,' Bobby wheezed. 'It was nice to see the NR3 through the carriage door at the end of the train.

That's my idea of a dependable locomotive. This futuristic stuff makes me nervous.'

'You crack me up, Bobby.' Karleen chuckled. 'You're the sweetest soul.'

'Let's see if there's any of that champagne left in the lounge,' Kenny suggested.

'Bet Leslie Deane's drunk it all,' Karleen said, waving cheerily at Nat, Hal and Marianne as they passed. 'She is a politician, after all.'

Bobby laughed and Kenny gave Woody a thumbs-up as he opened the door into the dining car. It clicked shut behind them.

'You don't really think someone on this train could be the person who cut those wires, do you, Hal?' Marianne asked. 'They would be putting themselves in danger.'

'We don't know what the saboteur's plan is. If they want to destroy the credibility of Boaz's train, it might not be dangerous. And we don't know if it's one person. It could be two, or more.' He sighed. 'You are right, though, those wires could've been cut before the train left the station by someone not on this train.'

Hal flicked back through the pages of his sketchbook, and then an idea occurred to him.

'Marianne, do you think you could draw the person who left the Rocket model for your dad? You're the only person who saw him. I think we can be certain he's involved in all of this.'

'I'm not like you,' Marianne protested. 'I draw cartoons, not real people.'

'Just try.' Hal passed her the pad and pen.

Marianne received them reluctantly, paused, then drew an oval for a head. She sketched in a nose, and started to shade in a beard, but then scribbled it out. 'No! That's all wrong.' She started again. After the third face had been scribbled out, Marianne let out a cry of frustration.

'*Urgh!* I can't do it.' She shoved the pad and pen back at Hal. 'When I try and draw him, the picture ends up looking like an angry garden gnome!'

'How about you describe him and I draw?' Hal offered, turning to a fresh page. 'Let's start with the face.' He drew an egg shape, then lightly quartered it. 'The eyes are halfway down the head. What did they look like? Were they close together or far apart?'

'Neither. They were normal. His eyes opened wide when he saw me, then he narrowed them.' She shuddered as she remembered. 'I think they were a dark colour, like brown, but I'm not sure. There were deep lines around them, but not friendly smile crinkles.'

Hal worked away at his drawing, ageing the skin around the eyes, making the lids heavy and the pupils dark.

'That's pretty good!' Marianne said, becoming excited. 'He had bushy eyebrows with grey hairs in. The grey hairs and the wrinkles around the eyes were the things that make me think the man was as old as Pop, or maybe older.'

'Good. Now, what about his nose?'

'His nose was straight, a bit bulb-like at the end, but not big. Below that was a moustache that went out as far as the edges of his mouth, and he had a neatly trimmed beard that covered his chin, but not the sides of his face.'

'A goatee? What about his hair? How was that styled?'

'He had a high forehead.' Marianne closed her eyes. 'His fringe was swept back from his face, showing a receding M-shaped hairline, and there were lines across his forehead.' She opened her eyes and pointed at the picture. 'In front of his ears – which were normal, they didn't stick out or anything – were neat sideburns that stopped before his ear lobes.' She paused and tilted her head. 'The moustache hid his top lip, but his bottom lip was visible.'

Hal worked away at the picture, giving the man a neck and marking in the porter's jacket.

'Oh! Hal! That's him!' Marianne whispered. 'That's the man that left the Rocket model at Pop's door!'

They both stared down at the picture.

'I've never seen him before,' Hal said with certainty.

'Woody, come look at this picture.' Marianne called the

bodyguard over. 'Have you seen this man?'

Woody and Uncle Nat crowded over the picture, but neither of them recognized the face on the page.

'I bet Pop will know who he is!' Marianne jumped to her feet. 'We have to go show him right now.'

CHAPTER FOURTEEN

TRUE LIES

'Come on.' Marianne grabbed Hal's sketchbook and rushed out of the observation pod. Hal got up to follow her and noticed that Uncle Nat and Woody were having a quiet exchange of words.

'Woody?' Hal pointed at the door. 'Marianne just left.'

Woody nodded at Uncle Nat, then hurried after Marianne.

'What were you talking to Woody about?' Hal was curious.

'We, er . . .' Uncle Nat stopped himself and sighed. 'I'm not going to sugar-coat this, Hal. You're not a baby. Woody and I have decided to work on . . . damage limitation.'

'What does that mean?'

'Michelle, Boaz and August are trying to take back control of the locomotive. You and Marianne are investigating who our saboteur could be. Woody and I . . . well, we're looking at worst-case scenarios and trying to, um, limit any damage.'

'By doing what?'

'By preparing for a crash,' Uncle Nat said bluntly. 'Until we can stop the train, we have to consider it as a possibility. The rear carriage is the furthest away from impact and therefore the safest. It has standard seats, which will give protection if people are in the brace position. We were discussing stripping the other carriages of all soft furnishings, to cushion any impact.'

'You think the train is actually going to crash?' Hal tried to swallow. His mouth was suddenly dry.

'No. That's not what I said. What I said was, we were running through worst-case scenarios and working out what we should do *if* we crash. It's a very big if. I trust August will find a solution, but *if* he doesn't –' he drew in a long breath – 'I want to have done everything I can to keep you safe.' He gave Hal an unconvincing smile.

Hal's stomach twisted. Despite all he and Uncle Nat had been through together, he'd never seen his uncle frightened – until now.

'Boaz will find a solution,' Hal said. 'I know he will. It's his train.'

Uncle Nat nodded.

There was no sign of Vincent or JJ as they passed back through the dining car, but the dessert trolley showed evidence of them having been there. The trolley held seventeen plates topped with cream-filled pastries drizzled in chocolate sauce. Four on the middle shelf had been pounded flat by a small fist. Cream was splattered everywhere. Hal paused, then took a cake from the top shelf and stuffed the whole thing into his mouth.

'Hal!' Uncle Nat exclaimed.

'If we are going to crash,' Hal mumbled, his mouth full of delicious chocolate and cream, 'then we should eat the cakes while we can.'

Uncle Nat stared at him for a second, then looked at the cakes. He picked one up, opened his mouth wide and put the whole thing in too.

They entered the lounge grinning, wiping chocolate from their mouths, only to find Marianne, Woody, Tom and Kira having a heated discussion.

'How dare you ask me that!' Marianne had one hand on her hip. The other was clutching Hal's sketchbook. 'Woody, punch him.'

'Now, now, I'm only doing my job. I'm a journalist,

remember . . .' Tom backed away, glancing fearfully at Woody, who didn't move.

Kira was grinning and pointing the camera at Tom, recording his grovelling on film.

'I apologize unconditionally.' Tom held his hands up as if Woody's glare were a gun, pointing at him. 'I thought you might want to tell the world *your* side of the story . . .'

'Well, I don't,' Marianne snapped. 'Stories don't have sides, and people who say they do are liars trying to make trouble.'

'Fine by me,' Tom babbled. 'Totally cool. Whatever you want.'

'Where's everyone else?' Uncle Nat asked, changing the subject.

'In the driver's cabin,' Kira replied. 'We couldn't fit. It's pretty crowded in there.'

'And you must be, ahhh . . .' Tom glanced down at the notepad on the seat beside him and read from the page. 'Nathaniel Bradshaw, the well-known travel writer!' He pointed his microphone at Uncle Nat. 'You must have some choice words for us. I'd really love to hear what you think of the Solar Express. Maybe you'd like to plug your new book too? An interview will only take ten minutes.' He smiled pleadingly, his eyes darting nervously towards Woody every few seconds.

'I don't have a book to plug right now,' Uncle Nat replied, 'but I'd happily talk to you about how much I approve of August Reza's pioneering vision and Boaz's inspired regenerative fuel cell. It puts me in mind of the condensing steam locomotive, turning used steam back into water to be sent through the boiler again, prolonging the length of time a train could travel without stopping.'

Woody relaxed and stepped back.

'Thank you,' Tom Flinch muttered. 'My life was flashing before my eyes.'

Marianne had gone to sit as far away from the journalists as possible. Hal dropped down beside her.

'We can't show Pop your drawing till everyone comes back out of the cabin,' she said with a heavy sigh.

'That doesn't mean we stop investigating.' Hal took the sketchbook from her and turned to the drawing of all the passengers. He looked up at the screen that showed the route to Tennant Creek. They were nearly a fifth of the way through the journey. 'We need to consider the motives and the means of everyone on this train.' He lowered his voice to a whisper. 'First, Tom Flinch and Kira Tate. Why might they sabotage the train?'

'Because they're dumb.' Marianne glared at them. Whatever Tom had asked her had really upset her.

'Or, perhaps, because Tom is hunting for a big story that will make the prime time news?' Hal raised his eyebrows, giving her a meaningful look.

'Oh!' Marianne perked up, remembering the scene they'd witnessed in the conference room the previous evening. 'Yes,' she whispered, 'So that he can get a job in London with the BBC?'

'And Kira wants to be a documentary filmmaker. Live

footage of a sabotaged train must be worth something.'

They stole a glance at the pair interviewing Uncle Nat, who was saying, 'Trains are already the most environmentally friendly way to travel. Making a transport system with zero carbon emissions is an admirable goal.'

'Do you think they'd do something dangerous for a story?' Marianne asked.

'It's possible. And they've had access to the train, to film it for their news piece. We should ask Michelle if they were on it this morning before the conference.' Hal pointed his pen at Michelle in his picture. 'And then there's Michelle . . .'

'Please say she doesn't have a motive. I like her.'

'You weren't keen on her babysitting you last night.' Hal laughed.

'Yeah, but that was before I knew she was a cool hacker.'

'And what kind of person got into the train's computers and sabotaged them?'

'. . . A hacker,' Marianne admitted.

'She had access to the train before departure,' Hal said. 'And she knows everything about this journey.'

'But she's trying to help us.'

'Or is she?'

'Wow. You suspect everybody.'

'Yes. Except Uncle Nat, and you.'

'Me?'

'From the moment we arrived in Alice Springs, you've been trying to make me see that something was going on. I should have listened to you. I'm sorry.'

'That's OK.' Marianne flushed pink and smiled.

'Now. What do you think of Kenny and Karleen Sparks?'

'I don't really know much about them.'

'Exactly. All we know is that they won the opportunity to ride on the Solar Express in a competition. They could be anybody.'

'Do you think the loud shirts and cheerful chatter is an act?' Marianne's eyes were wide. 'That, really, they're saboteurs?'

'I've been fooled by first impressions before. We can't take anything for granted. We need to get to know a bit more about those two.'

'What about the old train driver?' Marianne pointed at Bobby Benson.

'I can't think of why he would want to sabotage the train,' Hal admitted, 'but he did go to the toilet at the beginning of the journey. He could have crept into the driver's cabin and cut those cables.'

'Or, he could just be an old man that had to pee.' Marianne giggled. 'I can't imagine he'd be good at hacking computers.'

'Tell me about Francisco,' Hal said. 'He's the missing puzzle piece. I don't think it's a coincidence that he's the only person capable of stopping this train, and he isn't here.'

'I don't believe he'd ever do something like this.' Marianne shook her head. 'He and Pop fight, yes, but they make up too. They're like brothers. They don't always agree, but they love each other. And, I know Francisco would never do anything to hurt me. He's my godfather, and he's really kind, always taking my side when Pop's being strict.'

'That leaves Leslie Deane and Terry Chang.'

'They are very suspicious,' Marianne nodded. 'We should watch them.'

'We need to find out what they really think about the Solar Express.'

'We could ask Kira to show us the interview she recorded with them,' Marianne suggested. 'No one was in the carriage when they were interviewed. If either of them want Boaz's fuel cell to fail, we'll be able to tell from the things they say, and the way they say them. They are both powerful enough and rich enough to be able to sabotage a train.'

'And they'd be less likely to be suspected if they were on board when it happened,' Hal mused. 'Their defence would be that they'd never do anything to put themselves in danger . . .' He tapped his pen against his sketchbook. 'Let's see if we can get a look at that interview.'

CHAPTER FIFTEEN

NO TIME TO DIE

The group of passengers that had been visiting the driver's cabin trooped back into the lounge.

'That was amazing,' Karleen exclaimed to Kenny. 'A train as stunning as this one, that isn't going to pollute the planet in any way,' she enthused. 'If this is the future, then I'm buying a ticket.'

'Gotta admit, she's a beauty,' Kenny agreed.

'A train that doesn't need a driver! What is the world coming to?' Bobby Benson was muttering to himself and shaking his head as he hobbled to a chair and sat down. 'I like to drive with a hand on the throttle, an eye on the track, and using mechanical instruments, not screens.'

Kenny rubbed his stomach. 'Do you reckon it's nearly lunchtime? It's been a while since brekkie and I'm starving.'

Leslie and Terry came into the room looking thoughtful. August followed them into the lounge, talking. 'I really believe hydrogen is the future of the world's transport industry, because there is no cleaner way to power a vehicle.

The question is, do you want Australia to be at the forefront of this new industry, or do I have to go back home to America to achieve it?'

'Hydrogen isn't the only way,' Terry replied. 'Nuclear power provides a great alternative to fossil fuels.'

'Pop!' Marianne jumped to her feet, but he put his hand up, indicating that she had to wait.

'Because believe you me,' August went on, 'I'm going to invest every cent I have in making this work.' Putting his hand behind his back, so that his passengers couldn't see what he was doing, August pointed to the driver's cabin.

'Come on, Hal,' Marianne said with a huff. 'Let's go find Boaz.' She linked her arm through his and pulled him into the corridor. Behind them, August was cheerfully promising the other passengers that lunch was coming soon and suggesting they enjoy the observation pod, as if everything were going exactly as planned.

The door to the driver's cabin was closed, but Boaz opened it when he saw them approaching.

Michelle was leaning over the control desk, staring from one screen to another, tapping at buttons.

'How's she doing?' Marianne asked Boaz.

'Urgh!' Michelle made a frustrated noise. 'The new program is basic, but effective. All signals to the satellite are dead. The logins are corrupted. I can't see much else in the code, and I can't change anything. I'm trying to find a way to reconnect to the satellite, so we can get help.' She hammered a series of keys. 'Right now, no one knows the Solar Express has been sabotaged.'

124

'What does the code do?' Hal asked.

'It's a series of instructions to the train. I can get them up on this monitor. Look.'

Hal stared at strings of white letters and numbers that made no sense to him.

'The only noticeably strange thing is that the train's instructions don't seem to go beyond three hundred and ninety-three kilometres, but Tennant Creek is five hundred and nine kilometres from Alice Springs.'

'But that's great, isn't it?' said Hal. 'If the train is programmed to stop, that means it's not going to crash.'

'I didn't say it was programmed to stop,' Michelle said.

'Wait.' Boaz frowned. 'Can we see three hundred and ninety-three kilometres from Alice on a map?'

'Not on these screens,' Michelle replied.

'What is it?' Marianne asked Boaz.

'South of Tennant Creek is Karlu Karlu. I think that's where the train's program ends.'

'What's Karlu Karlu?'

'A sacred site, where gigantic round boulders are scattered around, some balanced on each other and some split clean down the middle. The white man name for them is Devils Marbles. The whole area is the traditional land of the Warumungu, Kaytetye, Alyawarre and Warlpiri people.'

'Why would the saboteur want this train to stop there?' Hal asked.

'I don't know.' Boaz rubbed the back of his hand across his forehead. 'But I don't like it.'

August came into the cabin. 'What did you want, Marianne?'

'Pop!' Marianne grabbed Hal's sketchbook from under his arm. 'Look, this is the man who delivered the Rocket model to the hotel room. Hal's drawn him. Do you recognize him?' She held it up.

Hal found he was holding his breath as August studied the picture.

'I'm sorry, pickle,' August sighed. 'I've never seen that man before.' He looked at Michelle. 'Any luck?' His expression fell as she shook her head. 'Blast,' he cursed quietly.

'Pop, are there any maps on the train – real paper ones?' Marianne asked.

'I don't know,' August admitted. 'There's a cupboard on that side of the cabin. There may be maps in there. Push the door. That's it.'

'A toolbox,' Boaz exclaimed, pulling out a red metal chest. 'That'll come in handy.' He smiled up at Michelle.

Marianne rummaged through a small stack of books and pamphlets, and found a dog-eared fold-out map. 'Look, it's got the route marked out in red,' she said, putting it down on the console.

'There, that's Karlu Karlu.' Boaz indicated the spot with his finger.

'That's where the train's program runs out.' Michelle nodded. 'But why?'

'I don't know.' Boaz frowned as he stared at the map. 'But I don't think it's so we can get off and appreciate a bit of Aboriginal culture.'

Hal stepped backwards, reeling at the realization that this attack was aimed at Boaz as much as August Reza. The person behind this sabotage was clever, calculating and very cruel. He felt a surge of anger. What kind of a creature would prevent the success of the Solar Express – a machine created for the good of the planet? And why? For money?

The only way to understand the saboteur's game is to play it, and beat them, Hal thought.

Going to the driver's private bathroom, beside the engine room, Hal went in and shut the door. Inside, he found the sink full to the brim with water and the Rocket locomotive submerged beneath it. This was the only clue they had to the identity of the saboteur. He leaned in close, examining every detail of the model.

You didn't go to the effort of making such a beautifully complex machine, announcing your intentions, but then not sign it, he thought.

'An artist always signs their work,' Hal muttered.

Was there something on the model that gave a clue to the saboteur's identity?

His eye snagged on a tiny groove on one of the tender wagon's wheels, which were above the

water as they weren't lithium. Then he saw that there was a groove on all four of the wheels. His heart skipped a beat. He turned the first wheel so that the groove was pointing to twelve on a clock, rotating the other wheels to match, but nothing happened. He turned each wheel so that the groove pointed to three on a clock. Nothing. Trying again, he made all four of the grooves point to six on a clock. As he turned the fourth wheel, he heard a click and gasped as the barrel on the tender wagon sprang open. The model train was a puzzle box!

Inside was a hidden compartment containing a small gold fox.

What does it mean? Hal wondered as he lifted out and examined the beautiful animal.

Putting the fox into his pocket, Hal continued studying the model. He had to be certain he'd discovered all its secrets.

Eventually, when he'd concluded

that there was nothing more the puzzle box could teach him, he headed into the lounge, to show Uncle Nat his discovery.

'I found something,' he said in a low voice as he sat down beside his uncle.

'What is it?'

Hal pulled the fox from his pocket, holding it under the table so no one else could see it.

'Ahh, *Vulpes vulpes*,' Uncle Nat said.

'What?'

'That's Latin for "red fox",' Uncle Nat explained apologetically. 'Where did you find that?'

'Inside the tender barrel of the Rocket model.'

Karleen, who had been watching the live feed from the front of the train on one of the screens, leaped to her feet. 'What the—! Kenny, *Kenny!*' she shrieked, pointing. 'There's a truck across the tracks!

Up ahead! I saw it on the screen! *Kenny!*'

The screen had flipped to the map graphic. Everyone pressed their faces to a window, but they couldn't see the tracks straight ahead.

Kenny yanked down a window and shoved his head out, leaning as far out as he could.

'There *is* a truck! It's not moving!' he yelled. 'Pull the emergency brake! Someone put the brakes on! There's gonna be a crash!'

CHAPTER SIXTEEN

FAST AND FURIOUS

'Nobody panic!' August appeared in the doorway of the carriage with his hands up. 'Does anyone know what road that is, up ahead?'

'Plenty Highway,' Leslie Deane snapped. 'State Route 12.'

'Excellent.' August clapped his hands together.

Everyone stared at him as if he'd lost his mind, including Hal and Uncle Nat.

'Please, relax. Sit down. In her earlier announcement Michelle neglected to mention this part of the Solar Express test run. I must admit that it had slipped my mind too.' He smiled. 'Things have been going so well, haven't they?'

Hal wondered what on earth August was doing.

'One of the biggest challenges of having driverless trains is the same as with driverless cars. What happens if there is an obstruction on the tracks? It could be an animal, a kangaroo perhaps, or –' he gestured to the screen – 'a stranded vehicle. You can see that the truck parked across the tracks, in the level crossing, is one of mine. It's a Reza

Tech truck. It has been put there on purpose.'

Hal read confusion on people's faces, but their panic levels were lowering and so were their shoulders.

August was right. The lorry stretched across the tracks had a silver awning with a large Reza Technologies logo written in orange and black.

'As we approach that truck, the Solar Express's sensors will detect the obstruction, and tell the computer to slow the train down.'

'The train will stop?' Vincent asked, sitting JJ on his knee, and opening one of her pop-up books. 'Phew, that's a relief.'

'Are you sure?' asked Bobby, leaning on his stick. 'We're going pretty fast. At this speed, it could take you half a kilometre to stop.'

'You mustn't worry, Mr Benson. Modern technology is capable of wonders.'

'Are you sure the sensors can detect an obstruction that far away?' Uncle Nat asked, looking uncertain.

'Absolutely. They've been rigorously tested,' August assured the room. 'The train's computers will have been informed that there is a possible obstruction from the satellite images that are fed to it as it journeys towards its destination.' He smiled, looking around to make sure everyone understood that everything was fine, and to Hal's surprise, everyone relaxed, returning to their conversations.

'Didn't Michelle say that all satellite communication was dead?' Hal whispered to Uncle Nat as August pivoted and returned to the driver's cabin.

Together they rose from their seats and followed August.

'What is going on?' Uncle Nat asked August, who was standing beside Michelle and Boaz, staring out of the windscreen of the train as it travelled towards the level crossing.

'We're being rescued,' August said, a smile playing across his lips.

'What do you mean, rescued?' Hal didn't understand.

'We would never build a test as dangerous as this into a journey with passengers.' August pointed at the approaching truck. 'There's only one reason that a truck of mine would be on the tracks, here, now, and that's because the tech team know they've lost control of the train. I don't know how they know, but they do, and they're trying to stop the train. Francisco's team built the train's sensors. He knows that this is a safe way of stopping it.'

'It's not going to work,' Uncle Nat said as they sped towards the truck. 'Bobby's right. We've got too much momentum to stop in time.'

'Trust the sensors,' said August, nodding reassuringly.

'Are you sure it's safe, Pop?' asked Marianne.

'We're not slowing down!' Boaz warned, looking at the speedometer. He glanced at Uncle Nat. 'We're still going full speed.'

'We're five hundred metres away!' Michelle stepped back from the screens.

'Hal, Marianne, get down on the floor. *Now!*' Uncle Nat ordered.

Hal was frozen to the spot, staring at the oncoming truck, his heart hammering.

Marianne looked terrified.

'*Get down now!*' Uncle Nat roared, and they both dropped to the ground.

Michelle curled up under the control desk and Hal saw that she was silently praying.

'Why isn't it stopping?' August cried. '*The train should be stopping!*'

'Hold on to anything you can,' Uncle Nat said, kneeling and gathering Hal and Marianne to him, so that his back was facing the windscreen and his body was shielding their heads.

Hal glanced up in terror as the orange and black logo of Reza Tech grew bigger and bigger in the engine's windscreen.

'STOP!' shouted August at the oncoming vehicle. '*STOP!*'

'Get down, Mr Reza!' Boaz dragged August to the ground, curling into a ball and covering both their heads with his arms.

An earth-shattering *BOOM!* shook the loco as it hit the truck. The impact threw Uncle Nat away from Hal, against the wall. Hal heard Marianne cry out for her dad. Images of Hal's mum, dad and baby sister flashed through his head as he squeezed his eyes shut.

At first his ears were ringing, but then he heard the high whine of the electric engine and the sound of wheels on tracks. Hal cautiously opened his eyes and found everyone else on the floor looking confused and frightened. 'What happened?' he found himself saying, even though he knew the answer.

'Are you hurt?' Uncle Nat asked him, getting up and dusting himself down.

Hal shook his head.

'Mari? Are you OK, Mari?' August was hugging his daughter to him.

'I'm fine, Pop. I'm fine,' came her muffled reply as she pushed her face into his chest, hugging him back.

Hal tried to get to his feet, but his legs felt like they were made of jelly. 'I'm OK,' he told his uncle, leaning back against the wall of the cabin. 'I think I'll just sit here for a bit.'

Uncle Nat helped Michelle up.

'The train blew the truck apart,' Boaz said in awe, looking out of the side window. 'It rode right through it. The cab is over there.'

From outside the train, they heard a loud explosion. Boaz ducked instinctively, and Hal saw a plume of flames shoot into the sky. Boaz straightened up, pressing his face against the window. 'It blew up!'

'Um, Mr Reza?' Michelle was back studying the screens in the control desk. 'I'm not sure why, but our speed is increasing.'

CHAPTER SEVENTEEN

SPEED

No one spoke. The atmosphere in the cabin was heavy. Hal thought he could taste fear in the air.

'The speed has levelled out at a hundred and thirty-six kilometres per hour,' Michelle said. 'We're going faster now.'

'August, get up.' Uncle Nat's voice was as sharp as a slap. 'You have to go into the lounge and explain the situation to the other passengers. They'll be frightened.'

August was sitting in a crumpled heap on the floor, looking dazed. He shook his head and hugged Marianne.

'He's right, Pop,' Marianne said, gently disentangling herself and getting to her feet. She held out her hand. 'Come on. I'll do it with you.'

There was a banging on the cabin door. Uncle Nat opened it. Kenny and Terry Chang were on the other side, looking angry.

'How dare you risk our lives with such a dangerous test!' Terry shouted.

'Not cool, bro.' Kenny was shaking his head angrily.

'Someone could've got hurt. What the hell was that?'

'It was *kinda* cool,' Boaz muttered, directing the tiniest of winks at Marianne.

'I, er . . . I don't know . . .' August said, still sitting on the floor. He looked at his daughter.

Marianne drew herself up to her tallest. 'On behalf of Reza Technologies, please allow me and my father to apologize to you, Mr Chang, and you, Mr Sparks.' She tipped her head in an expression of defiance that Hal had come to know well. 'Reza Tech owes everyone an apology and an explanation. We'd be grateful if you could ask all the passengers in the lounge to take a seat. We are dealing with an emergency situation. Everyone will need to be seated, and calm, for us to be able to give you all the facts.' The two men stared at Marianne. 'Once the group has all the facts,' she continued, 'we will decide how to proceed together. I think you'll agree this is the best course of action?'

'Yes, ma'am.' Kenny nodded.

Terry looked from Marianne to August, who, stirred into action by his daughter's display of leadership, was getting up off the floor. August met his eyes. Terry nodded and followed Kenny back into the lounge, but he didn't look happy.

'Well done,' Hal whispered to Marianne. She crumpled a little and gave him a grateful smile.

As they filed into the lounge, Hal and Uncle Nat sat down with the other passengers. Subtly, so no one would notice, Hal slid his sketchbook and pen from his pocket.

Boaz went straight to his dad, picking up JJ and

138

hugging her to his chest like a koala.

'Big bang and boom, Bo-bo!' she told him enthusiastically, clapping as he sat down beside his father. 'Boom again! Boom again!'

'What is going on, Mr Reza?' Leslie Deane's blue eyes were narrowed into a laser-like gaze.

August Reza looked around the carriage, and to Hal's horror he saw the man's lip wobble; he was clearly still in shock. 'I'm so sorry,' he half whispered.

'Reza Technologies is sorry,' Marianne said assertively, moving to stand in front of her father. 'We lied to you about the truck on the tracks being a part of the test run on the Solar Express. It wasn't. The truth is that, shortly after the train left Alice Springs, we became aware that the locomotive had been sabotaged.'

Karleen's hands flew to her face in shock. 'Sabotaged!'

… shortly after the train left Alice Springs, we became aware that the locomotive had been sabotaged.

'Yes.' Marianne took a breath, searching for the right words to explain what had happened, and shot Michelle a pleading look.

Michelle cleared her throat. 'The hard drive of the Solar Express has been hacked. All past logins are corrupted. The train's manual override and emergency brakes are . . .' She paused to choose her words carefully. 'Out of action. We can't reach the Reza Tech team, because connection to the Reza Tech satellite is down.'

'That sounds bad,' Vincent said, looking at his son.

'It is.' Boaz nodded.

'However, the good news,' Marianne said brightly, 'is that the Reza Tech team knows we've been sabotaged. That's why they put the truck across the tracks, to try to activate the emergency brake sensors and stop the train.'

'But it didn't work,' Terry said, 'because the sensors rely on satellite images to confirm an obstruction.'

'Yes,' Michelle agreed.

'We didn't tell you what was happening because we hoped that the truck would stop the train and you would all be able to get off safely, without causing unnecessary panic,' Marianne explained.

'And so you could hush up the sabotage,' Leslie muttered.

'When we hit that truck, I thought we were going to die!' Tom exclaimed to nobody in particular. 'I'm too young to die.'

'Where is Francisco Silva really?' Terry demanded. 'If he was on the train we wouldn't be in this predicament.'

'Who is Francisco Silva?' whispered Bobby to Karleen.

'The techie guy that built the train,' she whispered back. 'He's the brains.'

'I don't know where Francisco is,' August admitted wearily. 'No one has seen him today.'

'And you thought it was a good idea to go ahead with this test drive without him?' Leslie spat. 'The arrogance! It's your fault we're in this mess, and if—'

'Look,' Marianne said loudly, cutting Leslie off. 'I'm only thirteen years old and even I can see the best thing we can do is work *together* to stop the Solar Express. You grown-ups can argue and fight and blame each other if you want to, but I want to get off this train and go home!'

There was silence and Leslie looked at the floor.

Marianne took her dad's hand. 'Now, does anyone have any ideas about how we can stop this train safely?'

'Will you turn that *damn thing OFF!*' August growled at Kira, who was pointing her camera at him and Marianne.

'With respect, Mr Reza,' she replied, shaking her head, 'if some jackass is going to crash this train, and this is the last thing I ever get to film, then I'm filming till either the camera battery dies, or I do.'

This statement was greeted with silence, and August slumped into a seat.

'What about the NR3?' Bobby said. 'The diesel locomotive at the back of the train?'

'Yes!' Leslie exclaimed with relief. 'I'd forgotten about that. We've got another engine, and an engine driver.' She smiled at Bobby. 'Can we disconnect the carriages from the sabotaged locomotive and drive back to Alice using the NR3?'

'We could, but only if the train was stopped,' Bobby said.

'The NR3 was attached to the train as an afterthought,' August said, 'because Francisco thought the Solar Express would run out of power and need towing back to the station.'

'But it didn't,' Boaz said with a hint of pride.

'The NR3 is not connected to the Solar Express's air-brake system. It's attached with a buffers-and-chain coupling.'

'What does that mean?' Karleen asked.

'It's possible to disconnect the NR3 from the moving train, but not with the carriages,' Bobby said. 'We'll all have to squeeze into the cabin, which is small.'

Everyone looked at everyone else, adding up the number of people on the train and wondering how tightly they'd have to squeeze together to fit into the cab of the diesel engine.

'I'm not leaving the Solar Express,' Boaz declared calmly.

'What?' Vincent turned to his son.

'We can't leave an empty train hurtling out of control along the rail tracks,' Boaz said. 'People could get hurt.'

'If we're all off the train, I can call in the army to blow it off the tracks,' Leslie suggested, obviously excited by this idea.

'No,' Boaz said quietly. 'This is my train. I designed it. I will stop it.'

'How?' Terry Chang asked.

'Our braking system doesn't work. If it did, it would disconnect the fuel cell from the traction motor.' He nodded to himself as he was thinking. 'But *I* could do the job of the braking system. I could manually disconnect the fuel cell, by cutting the wires that deliver the electricity to the engine. If the engine has no electricity, the train will grind to a halt.'

'Would that work, Boaz?' Marianne asked, looking hopeful.

'That's freakin' dangerous, mate,' Kenny said, shaking his head. 'Those wires will be carrying a high voltage.'

'I know.' Boaz nodded.

'You'll need a second pair of hands to create the circuit break.' Kenny chewed on the side of his mouth. 'Once the wires are cut, they'll need to be wrapped with tape quick smart, to stop electricity from arcing between the live ends. You could get a serious shock. Might even start a fire in the engine room.'

'Kenny . . .' Karleen said putting a hand on his knee.

'Can't let the kid do it alone, hon.' Kenny put his hand on hers as he turned to Boaz. 'I'm a retired electrician. I'll help you.'

There was a murmur of approval.

'Retired?' Boaz asked.

'I won the lottery a few years back.' Kenny grinned. 'Karleen and me have been travelling the world ever since.'

'You haven't touched a circuit board in seven years!' Karleen exclaimed.

'Electricity don't change, darl.' He grinned at her. 'Anyhow, I can hardly walk around with a name like Sparks and not pitch in, can I? Dad'd never let me live it down.'

'Right, that settles it,' Boaz said. 'Kenny and I are going to try to disconnect the fuel cell. If we succeed, the train will

143

stop, we'll recouple the carriages to the NR3, and Mr Benson can drive us back to Alice Springs.'

'And if it doesn't work?' Leslie asked.

'We'll all have to try and fit into the NR3,' Boaz replied.

'I don't think this a good . . .' began Bobby, but Marianne stepped forward, silencing him.

'It will be far more comfortable to travel back to Alice Springs in the train,' she pointed out. 'And we may not all fit into the NR3.' She made a show of looking around the carriage. 'All in favour of this plan, raise your hand.'

CHAPTER EIGHTEEN

HAYWIRE

Hal noticed that the people who didn't raise their hands were Bobby Benson, Leslie Deane and Terry Chang. Bobby was muttering to Karleen that he thought they should jettison the Solar Express immediately and go home in the diesel loco. Leslie and Terry nodded their agreement. However, it was three against twelve, thirteen if you counted JJ, which Marianne did, and so Boaz and Kenny left the lounge car to see if they could get into the engine room and look at the fuel cell.

A glassy-eyed August Reza stood up. 'Anyone hungry?' he asked. 'I'm ravenous.' He rubbed his hands together. 'It's getting on for lunchtime. There's nothing we can do while they're working on the fuel cell, and it's a pity to waste good food.' He was smiling manically. 'Let's eat!' he declared, marching out of the lounge and into the dining car.

Kira, who'd been training the camera on August, followed him.

'Wait for me,' Tom said, chasing after her.

Marianne watched them go, looking worried.

'Actually, I am quite hungry,' Hal said, standing up.

'Me too,' agreed Uncle Nat.

Marianne shot them a grateful look.

The dining car was a monochrome design of black and white with art deco touches of gold around the lights and seat backs. The chairs and tables were dressed in white linen. Black rectangular slates were the centrepiece of each table, displaying pairs of pink and white sushi, sliced rolls of raw fish and rice wrapped in seaweed, and decorative flowers.

Hal could see August in the kitchen, at the far end of the carriage. He seemed to be searching the cupboards for something.

Kira had set her camera up on a tripod, and Tom was trying to draw August into a conversation. 'Mr Reza, what is the likelihood that the Solar Express might crash?'

Hal and Uncle Nat went and sat on a table for two opposite the World News crew, ready to intervene.

To Hal's surprise, Leslie, Terry, Bobby and Karleen came into the dining car and sat at a table.

'Kenny is a great electrician,' Karleen was saying proudly. 'That's how we met. My drongo of a brother flooded our bathroom. Water came through the floor, getting into the lights in the kitchen, blowing all sorts of fuses and stuff. When the electrician arrived to fix it, it was Kenny.' She picked up her chopsticks and helped herself to a piece of sushi from the black slate. 'I didn't need working lights to know he was a looker.'

'Do you think they'll get into the engine room?' Bobby asked Leslie and Terry.

'Doubtful,' Terry replied. 'The door is on the outside of the train. They're going to have to take a wall apart to get in there, but you've got to let the boy try and save his toy train.'

'Toy train is right.' Leslie snorted. 'And who put little Miss Bossyboots in charge?' She glanced down the aisle towards the kitchen. 'I don't know about you, but I think the grown-ups should be the ones making decisions at a time like this. We're on a runaway train, for goodness' sake, being driven by a computer! If I had my way, we'd all be in that engine at the end of the train already.'

'I agree.' Bobby nodded his head. 'I trust the NR3. It has controls and is fuelled by tried-and-tested, dependable fuel. I might go and take a look at it now.'

'Didn't Marianne say we mightn't all fit?' Karleen pointed out, dipping her salmon into a dish of soy sauce.

'How many people do you think you could fit into the cabin of the locomotive?' Leslie asked Bobby.

'There are two driver's seats, and a toilet, so that's three. You could probably fit another four people into the cabin, standing, and maybe another three in the vestibule. It'd be a bit of a crush.'

'That's only ten people,' Karleen pointed out. 'There are sixteen of us on this train.'

'I'm sure you could get a couple more in,' Terry said.

'Who are you planning to leave behind?' Karleen sat

back, looking at the three of them in disgust. 'Or are you volunteering to stay on the train?'

Hal nudged Uncle Nat, and whispered, 'Are you listening to what they're saying?'

Uncle Nat nodded. 'People show you who they really are when they're under pressure.'

Hal opened his sketchbook and nervously worked over the sequence of images he'd drawn capturing the moment when the train had crashed through the truck. 'What do you think the saboteur wants?'

'To destroy the Solar Express, I suppose.'

'Then why not just blow it up?' Remembering something, Hal put his pen down and slid his hand into his pocket, pulling out the golden fox. 'I think this is a clue to who the saboteur is. But I don't know what it means.' He doodled a picture of the fox on a clean page of his sketchbook. 'I keep thinking about that puzzle box. It would have taken a long time and a lot of money to make. You could own it for years without ever knowing there was anything to find inside it.' He looked at his uncle. 'If the saboteur planned to kill August Reza and everyone on this train, why give him a puzzle box that he might never solve?'

'You think the saboteur wants August Reza alive?'

'I don't know.' Hal shrugged. 'But I have got a horrible feeling there's more to come.'

'The saboteur would have been waiting for the moment that August realized the Solar Express had been sabotaged. But how would they know when that was?'

'When . . .' Uncle Nat paused, and Hal could tell that he was working through their journey so far. He looked at Hal. 'When we crashed through the truck?'

'When someone made an attempt to stop the train.' Hal nodded. 'Which is why we can cross Francisco Silva off our suspect list.'

'We can?' Uncle Nat picked up the gold fox. 'But he's got motive and means.'

'Yes, but if we agree the saboteur is *not* Francisco, then we must ask, *where is he?* Why didn't he turn up to the conference this morning? And how did the saboteur get his pass key? We know it must've been his key used to hack the onboard computer.'

'Yes.'

'Suppose Francisco was attacked, his key taken, and he was tied up somewhere. The saboteur would know that, eventually, Francisco would be discovered. The first thing Francisco would do is get the tech team to contact the train.'

Uncle Nat was listening intently.

'When the team realize the train is in trouble, they put a truck on the tracks.' Hal ran his pen around the drawing of the truck as the train hurtled towards it. 'That was the signal. That's what told the saboteur that everyone knew what they'd done to the train.'

'So that means . . .'

'Everything has gone to plan for the saboteur, and we have entered the next level of their game. The question is, what is it?'

Hal flipped his sketchbook pages to look at his drawings of the Rocket model. 'The puzzle box makes me think that this is personal.'

Uncle Nat handed the fox back to him and looked out the window. Narrowing his eyes and craning his neck, he stared up and Hal followed his eyeline. 'What on earth is that?'

'Drones! Reza Tech drones.' Hal sprang up. 'We should tell Marianne.'

Uncle Nat and Hal hurried back towards the driver's cabin. As they came down the corridor, they found Boaz on his knees with a spanner, removing the last nut from a white metal panel that Kenny was pulling away from the wall. It wobbled free, and Kenny carefully laid it on the ground. Marianne was standing in the driver's cabin, watching them work.

Michelle was back in the driver's seat, working away at the computer. She appeared to have constructed a tiny keyboard and wired it in underneath the desk.

'How are you getting on?' Uncle Nat asked.

'We're in,' Kenny replied, as Boaz clambered into the engine room. 'The entrance is on the outside of the train, which isn't much good when it's moving this fast, so we had to make our own door.'

Peering inside, Hal saw nine barrel-sized green and silver cylinders with *Tudawali RFC* written around the rim. 'Are they the fuel cells?' He was surprised. 'They don't look anything like the tank in your laboratory.'

'That was a prototype, a proof of concept. Each one of those tanks is made up of hundreds of these tiny hexagonal discs.' Boaz pointed at the nearest fuel cell. 'Each disc does the same job as the prototype. To convert enough energy to power a train, you need loads of them.' He drew Hal's attention to a row of silver cylinders strapped to the wall. 'That's the hydrogen.' He pointed to a huge metal rectangle at the other end of the room. 'Under there is the engine, the motor that's turning the wheels. And that is the generator.'

Kenny had already set to work taking the cover off the generator.

When he and Boaz lifted it free, Hal could see down into the whirring wheelbase of the locomotive.

'Before you go touching anything,' Kenny said, pulling his sunglasses from his shirt pocket, 'when working with live wires, you should wear rubber gloves, safety goggles, rubber-soled shoes and rubber-handled tools.' He put on his sunglasses. 'Got any goggles?'

Boaz shook his head. 'My boots have rubber soles.'

'Here.' Hal was surprised to see August standing beside him holding out two pairs of yellow washing-up gloves. 'I found them in the kitchen. Best I can do.'

'Take these.' Uncle Nat took off his glasses, blinking as he handed them to Boaz.

'I don't want anyone to get hurt,' Kenny said, 'so best not to have an audience.'

They all pulled away from the opening, but Hal was curious and lingered for a moment.

'It looks like this cable –' Kenny ran his finger along a thick wire – 'feeds power to the engine.' He handed Boaz a pair of wire cutters. 'I'll hold the wire. You cut. Try and make it quick and clean.'

Boaz nodded, and Hal could see he was nervous.

Kenny reached into his pocket and pulled out a reel of electrical tape. 'Once a Sparks, always a Sparks. You never know when you're gonna need tape.' He put the reel on to his thumb. 'Once the wire is cut, you fall back. I will wrap the end with tape. Got that?'

Boaz nodded again.

'Right. Let's do this.' Kenny held the wire taut, leaving a space for Boaz to cut, but then looked down, through the wheelbase of the train. He bent lower.

Boaz was concentrating on the cable between Kenny's fists. He opened the wire cutters and gripped the wire between the blades. Hal saw the muscles tense in Boaz's body as he prepared to cut the wire, and Hal moved away, back down the corridor. Then he heard Kenny yell.

'*WAIT! NO! STOP!*'

There was a blinding flash of light, followed by a shower of molten sparks. Boaz fell backwards into the corridor, landing on the floor, his hands up in front of his face.

Hal heard Kenny howl with pain. Then there was silence, and all he could hear was the sound of the wheels on the rails.

CHAPTER NINETEEN

THE WILD BUNCH

Uncle Nat and August rushed past Hal, who found himself moving backwards. Whatever had happened to Kenny, he didn't want to see it. Uncle Nat's glasses were lying smashed on the ground. Hal picked them up, feeling a ripple of shame as Marianne knelt beside Boaz, asking if he was all right. Boaz looked up at her, stunned.

'Kenny kicked me,' was all he said.

'He's unconscious,' Hal heard August say.

Woody and Michelle pushed past Hal.

'We need to get him out of here and into the kitchen,' Uncle Nat said, 'where there's space and cold water.'

Michelle suppressed a gasp as she looked into the engine room.

'Yes,' August replied, and there was a series of scuffling noises and a few grunts.

Boaz was on his feet. He and Marianne retreated to get out of the way, coming to stand with Hal.

'What happened?' Marianne whispered.

'I'm not sure,' Boaz replied. 'I was about to cut the wire, but before I could close the cutters, Kenny shouted, kicking me in the stomach. I let go of the cutters as I fell backwards. There was a burst of electricity.' He shook his head.

Woody and Uncle Nat came into the corridor. Each of them had a shoulder under one of Kenny's armpits, his arms hanging loose. Hal saw they were badly burned.

'Michelle, hold the doors and clear a pathway,' Uncle Nat barked, his voice strained from the effort of carrying Kenny.

'He's going to be OK,' August said to them. 'But we need to take care of his burns immediately.'

Hal, Marianne and Boaz followed at a distance, not wanting to get in the way. As they passed through the lounge car, Vincent put his hands over JJ's eyes, saying in a cheerful voice, 'Hey, JJ. I've got an idea. Do you want to play hide-and-seek with me?'

When the group entered the dining car, Karleen leaped to her feet.

'Kenny? *Kenny?*' Karleen looked at Michelle. 'What happened?'

'He's been badly burned,' she replied quietly.

Holding on to each other, Karleen and Michelle followed Woody, Uncle Nat and August into the kitchen.

'We need cold water,' Uncle Nat panted, as he and Woody gently laid Kenny on the floor.

Kenny groaned and Karleen looked like she might cry with relief. 'Babe, can you hear me?' She knelt beside him and everyone stepped away.

Michelle was in front of one of the big silver freezers. She pulled out an empty drawer and filled it with water from the cold tap. She and August carried it over, putting it on the floor beside Kenny, while Uncle Nat and Woody filled another drawer.

Lifting Kenny's blistering arm, August lowered it gently into the water. Kenny gasped with the pain and opened his eyes. Michelle received the second drawer from Uncle Nat and Woody and lowered his other arm into it.

'*Mmmmnnnnaarrgghhhh!*' Kenny clamped his teeth together at the pain.

Karleen knelt behind Kenny, lifting his head onto her knees, so he was sitting up a little, and babbled on and on about how much she loved him and what a ning-nong he was for messing with electricity.

Marianne had found a jug and a pile of tea towels. She passed them to Michelle, who wedged the towels under Kenny, and then using a third drawer of water, gently poured water over the burns on Kenny's neck and the side of his face.

'*Gahhhhhhh*,' Kenny cried out. 'That hurts!'

Hal stood watching the scene feeling utterly helpless.

'We're gonna need cling wrap for those burns once we've got the heat out of them,' Karleen said, taking off Kenny's necklace and slipping it into her pocket.

'I'll find some,' Marianne said, searching the kitchen drawers.

August stepped back. Hal could see the man felt responsible for what had happened to Kenny. The August Reza who had boldly told a room of journalists this morning that he was going to change the world looked haunted and broken.

'Mr Reza?' Leslie Deane was standing in the kitchen doorway. 'I think it's time we prepared the diesel locomotive, don't you? We must abandon this disaster of a train before more people get hurt.'

'I want to get off,' Tom nodded vehemently.

August looked at Terry, Tom and Bobby, who were stood behind Leslie, and he sighed, his shoulders slumping as he conceded.

'If I could get into the loco cab and take a look,' Bobby said. 'It's been a while since I've driven one, but it's like riding a bicycle. You never really forget.'

'Nathaniel,' August said. 'Can you take care of things here?'

'Yes,' Uncle Nat said, not looking up as he held back Kenny's shirt collar so Michelle could pour more water on his neck. 'We're fine.'

Marianne, who was using a saucepan to take cold water from the tap to refill the freezer drawer, glanced over her shoulder at the expressions on Leslie and Terry's faces. 'Take Woody with you,' she said.

Woody exchanged a look with Marianne and nodded.

As August passed Kira, who had focused her camera on the action in the kitchen, he muttered, 'Shame on you.'

Kira bristled but didn't reply.

Hal watched the group leave. Tom Flinch followed them, trying to get August to talk to him about the accident, but

August's mouth was clamped shut, his lips pressed together so hard they'd gone pale. Looking around the kitchen, Hal realized there was nothing he could do to help, and remembering the conversation he'd overheard earlier, decided to keep an eye on the group investigating the NR3.

Following at a distance, Hal watched Terry pause to let Tom catch up with him. Terry put his arm around Tom's shoulders, speaking softly to him as they walked. Tom frowned, then Terry put his hand into his pocket and drew out a clip of money. He gave the whole thing to Tom Flinch, who paused, before pocketing it and nodding.

Hal swallowed. Whatever he'd just witnessed wasn't good. Careful not to be seen, he waited until the group were amongst the luggage at the other end of the last carriage, before slipping in and clambering onto the nearest seat. Bobby Benson's stick was leaning against it and he was careful not to knock it over. Holding his breath, he peeped over the top.

'To get from here into the cabin,' August was saying, pointing through the window in the door at the far end, 'we have to step across the gap to that walkway, move along the outside of the loco, and go in through the door into the cabin. It's not safe to do it while the train is moving this fast.'

'We don't have much choice,' Leslie insisted. 'There is no way to stop this train.'

'Reza Tech will find a way to rescue us,' August insisted. 'We just need to sit tight and wait.'

'I'm not waiting,' Terry said. 'I want to get off this damn train.'

'I'm not driving that loco anywhere unless we take everyone with us,' Bobby insisted.

'Look, first we need to get into that cabin, see how many people it will fit, and whether Bobby can drive it,' Leslie snapped. 'Every second arguing is a second wasted.'

'We've got an injured passenger now.' Bobby was shaking his head. He looked distressed. 'How are we going to get him into the cabin?'

'We'll cross that bridge when we get to it,' Leslie said, putting a comforting arm around the old man.

'Leslie's right,' added Terry. 'Let's get into that cabin and then we can decide what to do.'

'Fine.' August sighed. 'I'll go first. Woody, could you help us get out of the carriage and on to the walkway?'

A blast of air rushed in as Woody opened the door, the sound of the train immediately louder. The strong man straddled the gap between the carriage and the NR3, one arm gripping the handrail of the loco, the other clamped to the door frame of the carriage.

As August stepped across to the walkway, he held on to Woody, until he'd got a firm grip of the handrail, the wind buffeting his clothes. Shuffling along, moving one hand over another, he made his way to the NR3 cabin door. Taking a bundle of keys from his pocket, he opened it and stepped inside.

'I'll go next,' Leslie said, glancing at Terry, 'then Bobby.'

She followed August, using Woody, but moving faster. Bobby was on the walkway before she was in the cabin. Then it was Terry's turn and lastly Tom's. Woody released his grip on the door frame, letting it swing shut.

Hal rushed to the other end of the carriage, looking through the window. Woody was stooping to get through the NR3 cabin doorway. He saw the big man stumble and crumple to the ground. For a second, Terry Chang was visible, standing over the bodyguard, a spanner in his hand. He dragged Woody into the cabin and closed the door.

Staring with horror at the space where Woody had been standing, Hal didn't know what to do. If he ran back to the kitchen to get help, he might be too late to stop whatever was happening in the NR3. He looked at the distance between the end of the carriage and the walkway. He thought he could make the jump. He opened the carriage door just as Tom Flinch came back along the walkway, gripping the handrail and looking like a windblown rodent. Tom was trying to shout something.

'What's going on?' Hal cried.

'Mutiny!' Tom cried. 'There's been a mutiny! Quick, go get help! Woody is hurt.'

Hal spun around, running through the carriage, then suddenly stopped as the image of Terry handing Tom the money clip popped into his head. He wrenched himself around to see Tom struggling with the coupling lever.

'No!' Hal cried, sprinting back to the doorway. 'Tom! What are you doing?'

'I'm sorry!' Tom yelled, straightening up as the chain dropped and the Solar Express moved away from the rolling

You idiot!
We can't leave them!

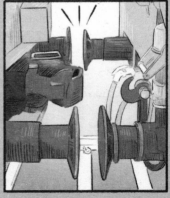

diesel locomotive. He shrugged, looking apologetic. 'I'm weak!'

Hal saw Bobby burst out of the cabin door in a rage, too late to stop what was happening. He ran down the walkway at an astonishing pace and roared at Tom. 'You idiot! We can't leave them!' He looked horrified as the gap between the Solar Express and the slowing diesel locomotive widened from ten to twenty metres, then thirty. Bobby shouted something to Hal, but the wind blew the words out across the Australian sands.

CHAPTER TWENTY

NO WAY OUT

As Hal made his way back to the kitchen, he struggled with how to tell the others what had just happened. He kept looking over his shoulder, expecting to see the diesel locomotive returning, but it was gone, and with it, Tom, Bobby, Terry, Leslie, Woody and August Reza.

'Where's Pop?' Marianne asked as soon as Hal appeared. 'Kenny has something urgent he wants to tell him.'

'Erm . . .' Hal looked at each of their expectant faces.

'What is it, Hal?' Uncle Nat asked. 'What's wrong?'

'The NR3, it's gone,' Hal stammered. 'Leslie and Terry did a mutiny. Terry knocked out Woody with a spanner. Tom released the coupling . . . They've all gone.'

There was a stunned silence as everyone took in this news.

'Tom's gone?' Kira looked disgusted, but unsurprised. 'That spineless toad! I knew he wasn't worth camel's spit.'

'They took the NR3?' Uncle Nat looked staggered that people could sink so low.

'I don't want to bum anyone out,' Kenny said, 'but I've got something worse to tell you.'

'What is it, hon?' Karleen said, stroking his hair.

'I wasn't going to tell everyone, just Mr Reza, but seeing as he isn't here, I guess this is all of our problem now.' He paused, obviously in pain. 'When Boaz was about to cut the power cable to the motor, I looked down, into the wheelbase of the loco. I saw . . .' He winced. 'I saw a dynamo attached to the train axle. It was connected to a box, strapped to sticks of dynamite.'

'A bomb!' Karleen exclaimed.

'Yeah.' Kenny closed his eyes, and everyone waited silently until he was ready to speak again. 'I only had a second to look at it, but from what I could tell, as long as the wheels are turning and an electric charge is being delivered to the bomb, it won't explode. But if Boaz had cut through that cable . . .'

'Kenny,' Michelle gasped. 'You saved our lives!'

There was a murmur as everyone in the kitchen understood what had happened.

'That's why you kicked me?' Boaz said.

'I kicked you to stop you cutting the wire, but you'd started. The electricity arced. It turned the cutters into molten metal.'

'Kenny, what did you do?' Karleen had tears in her eyes.

'I got the wire taped back up, didn't I?'

'You stupid . . . hero,' Karleen said, stroking his hair. 'You could've got yourself killed.'

'Nah, I'm too lucky for that. Anyway, I reckon the scars

will look great with my tattoos.' He tried to lift his arms and sucked air through his teeth at the pain.

Karleen was crying and laughing at the same time.

Hal found Uncle Nat was by his side, his hand on his shoulder. 'We're going to get through this, Hal. I promise,' he said calmly.

Hal found he couldn't speak. His chest was tight.

'Right,' Marianne said briskly. 'Karleen, we're going to leave you to look after Kenny for a bit, if that's OK? Everyone else, go sit down.' Marianne pointed to the dining car. 'We need to make a plan and it's going to have to be a good one.'

As he took his seat, Hal wondered how Marianne was feeling, knowing that her father and Woody had been ambushed. He guessed she was angry because she seemed very focused.

'Let's start with what we know,' she said, looking around the circle.

'The computer hard drive can't be accessed,' Michelle said, 'and I can't change the code, only see it. The computer controls the automated coupling system and the braking system. We can't uncouple the carriages or turn on the brakes.'

'Not that we want to, because if the train stops, it will trigger the dynamite and everything will blow up,' Boaz muttered.

'I can see that the computer program stops instructing the train over a hundred kilometres before Tennant Creek,' Michelle continued.

'In the Karlu Karlu national park.' Boaz shook his head.

'Why is that?' Marianne asked the group.

'If I were to hazard a guess,' Uncle Nat said, 'it would be that the track bends there. Our speed has been increasing the closer we get to Karlu Karlu. The faster a train is going, when it hits a bend, the more likely it is to derail.'

'That's why the computer program stops.' Michelle looked horrified. 'We're going to come off the tracks!'

'And if we derail, the wheels stop turning,' Boaz said.

He didn't need to go on. Everyone was imagining the train exploding.

Hal's body was leaden and heavy. He had been convinced that the saboteur didn't want to hurt them, but now he felt sick. There was a bomb on the train, and they couldn't stop it.

'Come and find me!' JJ shouted, bursting through the door from the observation pod. Vincent came in chasing her. Father and daughter paused when they saw the meeting taking the place.

'Last one into the lounge is a wombat!' Vincent said, chasing a squealing, giggling JJ through the dining car.

'Wait!' Hal sat up, suddenly remembering something. 'We forgot to tell you, Marianne. There are drones following the train.'

'What?'

'Uncle Nat and I saw them. They're Reza Tech drones. They may not be able to communicate with us, but they are following us. They can see us. They will have seen what happened with the NR3.'

'Yes!' Marianne exclaimed. 'We mustn't forget. We're not

alone. There are people out there trying to rescue us. We will *not* give up.'

Hal felt everyone's spirits lift.

Boaz got up and followed his father into the lounge. Hal guessed he was going to tell him what had happened.

'Hal, if there are drones with cameras following the train,' Marianne said, 'then we can put messages up in the windows. We can tell them what's happening. The more they know, the better.'

'I've got a flip chart and pens,' Michelle said.

'Can the two of you make signs to tell the drones that we've got an injured man on the train, and that they must *not* try and stop the train because of the bomb?'

'We can do that.' Hal nodded, relieved to be able to help.

He followed Michelle into the lounge and they got to work making signs for the windows.

As Hal finished one, Michelle taped it to the window with the message facing out.

Boaz was sitting bouncing JJ on his knee, talking quietly with his dad. Vincent was nodding and looking grave.

The map on the digital screen told Hal they'd completed more than half the journey. They couldn't be more than a hundred kilometres away from Karlu Karlu now. They had less than an hour till the Solar Express stopped.

'Vincent, I could do with your help,' Uncle Nat said as he and Marianne came in. 'We're going to turn the rear carriage into a lifeboat.'

'What do you need me to do?' Vincent said.

'I'm moving all luggage and loose items into the observation pod, and all soft furnishings, anything that might cushion impact, into the end carriage.'

'Sure.' Vincent got up and JJ slid from Boaz's knee.

'JJ help!' she said, looking very pleased with herself as she grabbed a white cushion from the seat beside her.

'I can help too,' Kira said, opening her camera bag.

'What are you doing?' Marianne asked.

'I'm stopping watching and starting helping.'

'You get that camera back out,' Marianne snapped. 'When we get out of this mess, I want evidence. I want everyone to see this. You make the best documentary you can, and I'll use it to make sure whoever did this gets put in prison for the rest of their lives.'

Kira nodded, pulling the camera back out.

'Boaz, Hal,' Marianne said. 'Can I talk to you?'

'Listen.' Marianne drew them to her in a huddle. 'I am giving everyone jobs. We need to keep spirits up and concentrate on getting as many people off this train as safely as possible. No ideas are stupid right now, so if you have any, even dumb ones, let me know.'

'This –' Boaz waved an arm – 'feels personal. I was talking with Pa and he agrees. Someone is really angry that it was *my* train that your father chose to invest in. The sabotage is cold and calculated. The track from Alice to here is a straight line, with barely a bend, but in Karlu Karlu the track curves and bends plenty. This train will crash there, the bomb will go off right under the hydrogen. It will make it a *really* big bang.'

'Why would anyone do that?' Hal said, aghast at the image forming in his mind.

'Because, if my locomotive explodes, scarring land sacred to Aboriginal people, my engine will be doing the opposite of what I designed it for. I'll be shamed. The reputation of hydrogen as a dangerous fuel will be reinforced. The Solar Express will be nothing but a boy's dream, and people will point to it as an example of why hydrogen-powered vehicles can never be trusted.'

'No.' There was fire in Marianne's eyes. 'That is *not* going to happen.' She turned to Hal. 'You are the detective. Work out who did this.' She pointed. 'Sit there and draw until your fingers fall off.' She looked at Boaz. 'And don't you dare let this train fail. *You* won the competition, not whoever did this, and that's because you are smarter than they are. You've got to out-think them. OK? You've done it once, now do it again.'

'You're feisty, aren't ya?' Boaz chuckled. 'Wouldn't want to let you down.'

'You're not going to,' Marianne said without a hint of humour. 'Neither of you are.' And with that she marched out of the carriage.

CHAPTER TWENTY-ONE

CLEAR AND PRESENT DANGER

Hal and Boaz sat down at two tables next to one another. Hal took out his sketchbook and pen. Boaz had torn a sheet of paper from the flip-chart and pulled a pencil stub from his pocket. The two boys looked at their blank pages, then at one another.

'Marianne is smart,' Boaz said. 'If she keeps everyone busy, no one has time to think about the fact that we're sitting on a bomb.' He drew a diagram of a wheel axle with a dynamo connected to it. 'And one of us might actually come up with a way out of this mess.' He drew a wire delivering an electric charge to a box and then two curling wires joining it to three sticks of dynamite. He stabbed his pencil at the diagram. 'I've gotta deal with the bomb first. Get rid of it. Remove it from the equation. Then I can stop the train.'

'If you move the bomb away from the wheel axle, won't it think the train has stopped and blow up?'

'The electric charge from the dynamo stops the fuse box

from igniting the dynamite.' He chewed the end of the pencil, thinking. 'If I can estimate the voltage of the charge, I could attach a new power source.' He looked at Hal. 'If the bomb had a different power source – a portable power source, like a battery – we could detach it from the loco and move it.'

Hal felt hope flare in his chest. He wanted to be as far away from that bomb as possible. Its presence was oppressive. He felt like it was crushing his brain into a tiny box labelled *Fear*.

He opened his sketchbook at the first page, staring at drawings of the kangaroos he'd done only the other day. It felt like a year ago. Slowly and thoughtfully, he turned the pages.

He felt a pang when he saw his first drawing of Kenny declaring how lucky he was, and thought of the man now lying on the kitchen floor.

He wished he'd listened to Marianne as soon as she'd told him about the mysterious man who'd delivered the puzzle box to August Reza's hotel room. If he'd worked out the message in the Rocket model before they'd got on the train, he might have been able to stop all of this from happening.

Putting his hand in his pocket, Hal took out the golden fox. He stared at its face. What did it mean? Foxes were known for their cunning, their cleverness. He turned the fox over in his hands, scanning every millimetre of it, and then he noticed something. There was a tiny stamp on the underside of each of its paws. At first he thought it was a hallmark, but then saw that three of the feet had a tiny *H* preceded by numbers, while the fourth paw had a tiny *GV* engraved on it. He frowned. 'Boaz, do you recognize these symbols?'

Boaz looked up from his paper, where he'd drawn a series of diagrams with boxes, arrows, pluses and minus. He squinted at the fox. 'Those look like . . . tiny nuclear symbols for the isotopes of hydrogen.' He frowned. 'But I don't know what the *GV* is. What are they doing on the feet of a fox?'

'I found the fox inside the model of the Rocket.'

'That thing was dangerous,' Boaz said, returning to his workings out.

'You said sabotaging the train felt personal, like it's an attack on you and August. I think you're right.'

'Yeah?'

'What if the saboteur is someone who didn't win the Reza's Rocket competition? Someone who thinks they're clever, that their idea is better than the Solar Express? Someone who is furious that they didn't win, that they lost to a child, and wants revenge?'

'Then I'd say they were a bloody sore loser and a nasty piece of work!'

'And what if –' Hal tilted the fox so Boaz could see the paws – 'the design was for a nuclear-powered train?'

'There *was* an entry for a train powered by a nuclear reactor!' Boaz's brown eyes widened. 'August said it was crazy dangerous. He was worried terrorists might try and steal the nuclear reactors out of those trains and turn them into weapons. And, of course, there's no green solution to disposing of nuclear waste.'

Hal flicked to the impression he'd drawn of the man who delivered the Rocket model. 'I'll bet this is the person who designed it. Question is, how did he get on to the Solar Express to sabotage it?'

Turning to a fresh page, Hal began drawing a picture of himself thinking. Moving into the state of mind in which he drew calmed him. It was like meditation. As his pen stroked the page, he let his brain gambol through everything he'd seen and drawn since he'd arrived in Alice Springs.

He expanded his sketch, drawing Boaz working beside him. Hal thought about everything this day should have been for the young inventor: a triumph, a celebration. Hal's fear was eclipsed by anger. Some humans were so selfish. What kind of a person would be prepared to endanger the lives of innocent people to destroy someone else's invention? To wreck a young person's victory? And like a diode on a circuit board, this thought directed the current of his logic to flow in one direction. He flicked backwards, then forwards through his sketches, and gasped as a lightbulb illuminated in his mind.

Boaz grabbed Hal's arm. 'If we can get that bomb off the train –' he looked excited – 'I might've come up with a way of stopping the Solar Express before it hits the bending track in Karlu Karlu.'

'Is it dangerous?' Hal asked.

'Of course it's dangerous,' Boaz replied happily, slotting his pencil stub behind his ear.

'Guys!' They both looked up to see Kira running into the carriage. 'There are three red utes driving up behind the train.' She looked euphoric.

'What's a ute?' Hal asked Boaz.

'A utility vehicle. You know, a pickup truck.'

Kira clapped, bouncing on the balls of her feet. 'I think we're being rescued!'

CHAPTER TWENTY-TWO

CONVOY

Boaz and Hal hurried after Kira, through the train to the last carriage, which was now strewn with cushions and fabric. Kenny was perched on the edge of one of the seats. His shirt was hanging loose, and underneath, Hal could see that his arms, his torso and his neck were wrapped in layers of cling film. He was holding himself stiffly, wincing when he moved, but when he saw the boys, he smiled.

'Looks like it's time to abandon ship,' he said cheerfully.

Uncle Nat and Vincent had opened the rear carriage door, and through it, approaching fast, Hal could see three red pickup trucks.

Standing on the trailer of the middle truck, leaning forward over the cab, was a man gripping a loudhailer. 'G'day!' he called. 'We heard you need a lift outta here!'

Everyone in the carriage cheered.

As the trucks got closer and closer, Hal could see that the middle truck was being driven by a muscly woman in a white vest, and the other two by men in black T-shirts, one of whom was wearing his cap backwards. All three drivers were wearing sunglasses and determined expressions. Hal's heart fluttered at the sight of them, and he sat in a seat, to draw them.

Michelle passed Uncle Nat the cardboard back of the flip chart, which she had rolled into a funnel and taped up.

'We've got an injured man and four children on the train,' Uncle Nat shouted.

The man with the loudhailer gave Uncle Nat a thumbs-up. 'We can't come alongside the train. The ground is too bumpy,' he said. 'There's no safe way to get you off.' He paused to make sure Uncle Nat had heard him. 'We're going to take you off through this door. Mandy is going to do a one-eighty and reverse, to get the flatbed as close as possible to the door, but you're going to have to jump across the gap.'

There was a long silence as everyone in the carriage thought about how risky that jump was.

'Back in a sec,' Boaz said to Hal, disappearing into the observation pod.

The three trucks diverged, and the one carrying the man with the loudhailer did a handbrake turn. He held on as it spun, so that the rear of the ute was facing the train. Then it reversed on to the train tracks, positioning itself so the rails passed between its wheels.

From this angle, Hal could see that the man with the loudhailer was attached to the cab with a harness.

'It's not going to be able to reverse up to the train,' Vincent said, as the truck fell back. 'Reverse is a low gear. The train's travelling too fast.'

A second truck drove on to the tracks, facing forwards, accelerating until it was nose-to-nose with the reversing truck, touching bumpers.

'She's putting it in neutral,' Uncle Nat said, looking impressed as the two drivers executed the manoeuvre. 'The truck at the back is pushing the reversing vehicle.'

There was a roar as the second truck accelerated aggressively, pushing the reversing ute closer and closer to the carriage door.

Boaz burst back into the carriage carrying the metal panel that he and Kenny had removed to get into the engine room. 'Gangplank!' he said, bringing it forward.

Everyone cheered.

'Nice one!' Kenny declared, and Hal felt all their spirits lift.

For the first time since they'd discovered the sabotage, he could see a way out of this terrifying situation, and it made him giddy.

As the ute inched closer, Uncle Nat and Vincent laid the metal panel flat on the floor, carefully feeding it out of the door.

The man with the loudhailer had put it down and was crawling to the back of the truck, letting his harness strap feed out little by little.

'Nice to meet you all,' he shouted cheerfully. 'My name's Paul.' He pointed to the truck drivers. 'That's Glen, Josh and Mandy. We're from the Alice Springs Fire Department.' Gingerly he reached out and grabbed the other end of the metal panel, pulling it over the lip of the trailer and holding it down. 'Right, who's coming off first?'

'Kenny, Karleen,' Uncle Nat shouted. 'You're first.'

'How d'you want to do this, babe?' Karleen asked, looking frightened but resolute.

'You go first,' Kenny said. 'I'm gonna need your help.'

Karleen nodded. She gritted her teeth, got down on her hands and knees and crawled out on to the metal sheet, gripping the sides. Halfway across, she closed her eyes, unnerved by how the surface bounced as the truck bumped over the railway sleepers, but Paul was talking to her constantly, encouraging her. Hal could see she was scared, as the wind buffeted her, but Paul was there. He took hold of her wrists as soon as she was close enough, putting her hands on to his shoulders, then he grabbed her waist, holding on to her as she tumbled into the trailer.

'You little ripper!' Kenny whooped, delighted to see Karleen safe in the truck.

'Your turn,' Uncle Nat said to him.

'Mate, I can't hold on to anything with these,' Kenny held up his blistered cling film-wrapped hands. He could not make his way across the gangplank the way Karleen had. 'I'm going have to make a run for it.'

Hal stared at him in horror. 'But you'll fall!'

'Don't worry,' Kenny replied with a wink. 'Lady Luck loves me.'

He turned and walked to the end of the carriage to get a run-up, while Uncle Nat explained to Paul what Kenny was about to do.

Paul got Karleen to kneel on the opposite side of gangplank to him. He attached a harness around her waist and clipped it to the side of the truck.

Everyone drew back in silence, their expressions tense. Hal's heart was beating so hard he thought it might burst out of his chest. He caught his breath as Kenny burst into a run.

Everything moved in slow motion. Kenny's face was a picture of determination as he hurtled out of the carriage door, slamming his feet on to the gangplank and hurling himself forward, relying on momentum to carry him into the trailer. Paul and Karleen's arms reached up, grabbing him, and tried to turn him as he slammed down on the floor, hitting the trailer-bed on his side, crying out as one of his burned arms hit the deck.

Kenny's eyes were squeezed tightly shut, his teeth clenched and his knees curled up protectively. Karleen was talking to him, but Hal couldn't hear what she was saying.

After a moment, Kenny nodded and opened his eyes. Karleen and Paul helped him to sit up and moved him, so he was leaning against the cab.

Kenny grimaced at the anxious faces peering at him from the train, trying to smile.

'OK, Vincent, you and JJ are next.' Uncle Nat said. 'Boaz, come and hold the gangplank for your dad.'

JJ was standing beside Boaz. She took his hand and shook her head vehemently. 'JJ not do it.' She looked terrified.

Kira put down her camera and picked up a tablecloth from a pile of them on the floor. 'Don't worry, JJ,' she said. 'We're going to make a sling for you. You can hide in the sling while your dad carries you.' She brought two opposite corners of the square cloth together and tied them in a knot, testing it to make sure it held.

Vincent knelt in front of JJ. 'Pa's big and strong.' He thumped his chest like a gorilla, and she giggled. 'I'm going to carry you, JJ. It's gonna be fun, just see.'

Kira looped the tablecloth over Vincent's head, turning it into a giant sling coming over his broad shoulders. 'JJ, can you sit in here?' She pointed.

JJ nodded, clambering in.

'That's it,' Kira encouraged her. 'Stick one leg out each side. Well done. Isn't that cosy?' She reached down and grabbed a reel of gaffer tape from her camera bag. 'Now cling to your daddy, like a koala cub. You got that?'

JJ nodded, wrapping her arms around Vincent's neck and legs around his ribcage.

Kira pulled at the end of the gaffer tape, sticking it to the tablecloth supporting JJ's back. Then she wrapped it round Vincent's torso and back round JJ, again and again, until the whole roll was gone.

Vincent stood up, testing the sling and nodded gratefully at Kira. 'That feels good.' Approaching the gangplank, he put a hand on Boaz's shoulder. They exchanged a look but no words.

'Are you ready, JJ?' Vincent said in a cheery voice. 'Here we go.' He got down on his hands and knees. 'Hold on tight. That's it. Now. Close your eyes. This is gonna be over real

181

quick.' Gripping the edges of the metal sheet so hard that his knuckles were white, Vincent, calmly and with stoic determination, crawled out of the carriage towards the flatbed.

Hal saw the metal bow under their weight.

Kenny shouted encouragement as Paul and Karleen helped Vincent off the gangplank. He made his way to sit beside Kenny, hugging JJ, whose head was poking out of the sling, looking delighted.

'We can fit two more,' Paul shouted. 'Then we'll have to change over to the other truck.' He pointed at the third red ute keeping pace with them beside the tracks.

'Hal?' Uncle Nat looked at him.

'I want to go in the next truck, with you.'

'Right, Marianne, you're up,' Uncle Nat said.

'Michelle goes before me,' Marianne replied. 'She's a Reza employee. It's my responsibility to make sure she gets off this train safely.'

Michelle looked surprised and turned to Uncle Nat to protest, but he waved her forward.

'Go on, Michelle,' Marianne said with a curt nod, and Michelle's resolve crumbled. She kicked off her shoes, dropped to her knees and crawled on to the gangplank. She let out a panicked exclamation at the strength of the wind, but Paul leaned out and grabbed her wrists, pulling her towards him, manoeuvring her into the trailer in the same way he had Karleen.

Uncle Nat turned to Marianne.

'I'm going last,' Marianne said, in a tone that declared

it was pointless arguing with her.

'*I'm* going last,' Boaz said. 'This is my train.'

'I think you'll find . . .' Marianne faced him, ready for a quarrel.

'We have a problem.' Uncle Nat raised his voice. 'For the gangplank to hold steady, there need to be two of us holding it. There are five of us left. Three more can cross, but then we'll have to find another way on to the truck.'

'I'll hold it with you,' Kira said to Uncle Nat. 'We need to get the children off.'

'No. I'm staying,' Boaz said. 'I have to stop the Solar Express derailing. The explosion will devastate Karlu Karlu. I can't let that happen.'

'But there's no way . . .' Kira started to say.

'There is,' Boaz replied calmly. 'I've worked out a way.'

'What is it?' Marianne asked.

'If I can get the bomb off the train,' Boaz replied, 'I'm pretty sure I can stop the Solar Express.'

'Don't you understand how serious this is?' Kira looked horrified. 'This is not a game. You could die.'

'That's the thing,' Boaz said. 'For the sicko that sabotaged this train, this *is* a game.' His nostrils flared with anger as he slowly shook his head. 'And I'm not about to lose.'

'Me neither,' Marianne agreed.

'Hal?' Uncle Nat asked.

'I'm staying too.'

'So, who *is* getting into the truck?' Uncle Nat asked.

'Kira,' Boaz and Marianne said at the same time.

WROOOOOOM

Kira looked at them as if they were mad.

'I'll keep filming for you,' Marianne offered, 'if you want to give me your camera.'

Kira looked at Uncle Nat, handed her camera to Marianne, and dropped to her knees. As she shuffled on to the gangplank she said, 'You're all crazy.'

Once Kira had made it safely to the trailer, Uncle Nat and Boaz retracted the gang plank.

'Hang on tight,' Paul shouted to his passengers.

The ute pushing the reversing truck dropped back. Mandy put her truck into forward gear and drove off the tracks and away from the train, before coming to a stop alongside another of the trucks. Paul jumped out of the trailer full of passengers, slapping the truck on the side. Hal watched as it drove away in a cloud of dust, heading back to Alice Springs.

'And then there were four,' Uncle Nat said.

'The fabulous four,' Marianne said, panning the camera around and focusing on Boaz. 'Tell us, what's your plan?'

'You'll see.' Boaz leaned out of the carriage doorway, waving at the driver of the third ute, who was still following the train on the tracks. The driver accelerated, held the steering wheel steady and poked his head out of the window.

Boaz grabbed the funnel and shouted, 'I need to blow up one of your trucks!'

CHAPTER TWENTY-THREE

BATTERIES NOT INCLUDED

'Boaz!' Uncle Nat grabbed his arm, pulling him back from the carriage door, looking horrified. 'What are you planning to do?'

'Move the bomb,' Boaz replied calmly. 'I can do this. I'm going to create an alternative power source for the fuse box. All I need is a battery and wires from the driver's console. We can get the bomb off the train by putting it into the back of one of those trucks. They can drive it out into the bush and blow it up.'

Hal studied Uncle Nat's face as he struggled with the fact that this idea made sense but was also very dangerous.

'Hal, there's no need for you or Marianne to stay,' Uncle Nat said, looking at him. 'I'll help Boaz.' He pointed to the red truck following the carriage. 'If one of the trucks is used for bomb disposal, there'll only be one truck left. It won't be able to reverse up to the train. We won't be able to get off. So you must get off now.'

Hal moved towards Boaz, and Marianne did the same.

'We're sticking together, Mr Bradshaw,' she said, pointing the camera at him. 'Boaz needs us. It's going to take all of us. We're a team. You can go if you want.'

'I'm not going anywhere!' Uncle Nat spluttered. 'I'm not leaving you on a runaway train *with a bomb*!'

'Good, then let's get to work,' Boaz said. 'We don't have much time, about forty minutes by my reckoning. I need you to find me a battery or something that will deliver an electric charge.'

Uncle Nat went to the carriage door, shouting to the driver of the ute to drop back and follow the train.

Hal thought about all the things he had at home that were powered by batteries – the TV remote control, Bailey's dog flap, his lightsaber. None of them could be found on a train. He decided the kitchen would be a good place to look for batteries and dashed through the observation car to find Marianne already there, pulling out drawers, letting cutlery and implements drop to the floor.

'Any luck?' Hal asked, joining her, opening and closing cupboards.

'Not yet!' Marianne had a look of fixed concentration on her face. 'Who knew it would be so hard to find a battery?' She paused, staring at a rectangular silver tea-tray. Grabbing it, she muttered, 'That will come in handy.'

Uncle Nat and Boaz were in the driver's cabin. Boaz was lying on his back on the floor, his head under the console desk.

'Boaz, there are no batteries on this train,' Marianne said, exasperated. 'Everything is powered by the solar panels on the roof! That's the whole point of your design!'

'Wait!' Hal said, looking around. 'Don't train drivers have emergency kits? Won't there be a torch in it? We can take the battery from that.'

Marianne looked at him, waiting for the penny to drop. 'There *are* no train drivers on the Solar Express!'

'Yeah, I think I might ask Francisco to change that in the next version of the prototype,' Boaz said. 'Drivers feel pretty essential right now.'

Hal's spirits were sinking as he racked his brains trying to think of where they might find a battery and drawing a blank.

'*Aargh!*' Uncle Nat yelled, jumping as if he'd experienced an electric shock. '*My watches!*' He yanked back his shirt sleeves so they could see the three wrist watches he wore on each arm. 'Each one has a battery in it!'

They looked hopefully at Boaz.

'One won't be powerful enough on its own, but six . . .' Boaz grabbed Uncle Nat's extended wrist, and then looked quizzically at him. 'Who wears six watches?'

'An idiosyncrasy of mine,' Uncle Nat replied with a grin. 'I'd happily give them up to save the train.'

And all of our lives, Hal thought.

'You don't need to give up the watches,' Boaz said. 'Just the batteries.'

They sprang into action. Uncle Nat took off the six watches while Hal rummaged through the toolbox, pulling

188

out the smallest screwdrivers, then took them to a table in the lounge.

'Hal, I didn't want to say anything before, and I don't want you to be alarmed,' Uncle Nat said in a low voice, 'but without my glasses, I can't see where the screws are.' He lay the six watches face down on the table-top. 'Anything closer than a metre is a complete blur.'

'I can do it,' Hal said, suddenly remembering Uncle Nat's smashed glasses.

Leaning over to study the backs of the six wrist watches, Hal noticed all six were different. Uncle Nat handed him the tiny screwdriver and a focused surgery began. Hal carefully prised open and unscrewed the watches, revealing the six silver coin cell batteries nestled in their mechanisms. He took them out, one by one, as Boaz came in with a handful of wire he'd stripped from the driver's console.

Marianne put the empty silver tray down on the next table, as Hal was reassembling Uncle Nat's watches.

'What's the tray for?' Boaz asked, selecting a long piece of wire.

'The bomb,' Marianne replied. 'The most likely thing to set it off is if it gets knocked or jolted and the connection to the electricity is cut. That's why we need the tray. Once you detach the dynamo, you can carefully lift the bomb on to the tray and carry it through the train.'

'Nice one!' Boaz smiled at Marianne. 'I hadn't thought of that.'

Marianne shrugged, trying to act casual, but as she turned

189

away, Hal could see she was flushed with pleasure at Boaz's praise.

'I'm going to need cling wrap,' Boaz said, taking a penknife from his pocket and stripping the casing from the ends.

'On it!' Marianne rushed to the kitchen.

Boaz folded and wrapped the bare leads around the insulation several times, turning the ends into connectors.

Marianne arrived back with the roll of cling film and a pair of scissors. 'There's only a tiny bit left,' she said.

'I only need a thin strip.' Boaz held up his forefingers. 'Cut me a piece about one centimetre wide by about fifteen centimetres.'

Hal watched with interest as Boaz checked each coin cell battery, making sure he stacked the positive side on top of the negative side, forming a tiny tower. He held his hand out for the cling film, and Marianne supplied the strip.

Boaz placed the strip of film on the table and lifted the tiny stack of batteries on to it, wrapping it over and over the battery tower. He picked it up between his thumb and forefinger. Hal thought they looked like a packet of silver Swizzels Fizzers, his favourite sweets.

'Time for a trip to the kitchen,' Boaz said, getting up. 'Marianne, turn on one of the electric rings. Hal, I'm going to need a pair of tongs. Mr Bradshaw, can you bring the wire?'

Marianne and Hal scurried ahead of Boaz, kicking a path through the cutlery and pans they'd turned out of the drawers and cupboards in their hunt for a battery.

Grabbing up a pair of rubber-handled tongs from the

floor, Hal held them out as Marianne turned on a ring on the stove top.

Boaz was so calm and focused that Hal found it mesmerizing to watch him place the cling film-wrapped battery stack into the jaws of the tongs and hold it over the heat. The cling film shrank, binding the battery stack together.

Taking the bundle of wire from Uncle Nat, Boaz fed the silver ends under the cling film, one to each end of the battery. He briefly held the tongs back over the heat, so that the film shrank even more, holding the wire connectors tight to each end of the battery stack.

'You beaut!' Boaz said, dropping it into his palm and dashing back to the lounge car.

Throwing himself back into his seat at the table, he stripped the other end of the wires that were now connected to the battery stack. He looked around, frowning.

'What is it?' Marianne asked.

'I need two alligator clips. I've made them in the past with clothes pegs, paper clips and a bit of tinfoil, but I don't think we're going to find clothes pegs on the train.'

'Hair clips!' Marianne shouted, spinning round and running out of the carriage.

'I hope that means she has some,' Boaz said to Hal.

'I don't want to alarm anyone,' Uncle Nat said, narrowing his eyes as he stared at the screen with the route map on it. 'But we're about thirty minutes away from Karlu Karlu.'

'Here!' Marianne sprinted back into the carriage holding a packet of six silver, pincer-like hair clips. She was gasping for breath. 'In my washbag . . . in my suitcase.'

'Yes, Marianne!' Boaz's face lit up. 'They're perfect!'

He attached the clips to the bare wires, twisting them around to make a firm connection. Then he put the battery stack, the wires and the clips on to the tray.

Taking a deep breath, Boaz looked at each of them and said, 'Right then, let's go move that bomb!'

CHAPTER TWENTY-FOUR

COLLATERAL DAMAGE

Boaz went first, carrying the tray. Uncle Nat, Marianne and Hal followed behind, walking solemnly down the corridor towards the engine room.

Stepping inside, Boaz set the tray down on the floor, kneeling beside it while Uncle Nat lifted the casing off the generator. Hal could see the wire that Kenny had wrapped with electrical tape.

'I'm gonna need you to hold my calves. Make sure I don't fall down the hole,' he said to Uncle Nat, who nodded, then crouched down beside him.

Standing outside the gap in the wall, Hal and Marianne peered in.

Boaz sucked in a deep breath and leaned his head down for a clear view of the bomb.

Hal glanced nervously at Marianne. She took hold of his hand and squeezed it.

Uncle Nat's eyes were fixed on Boaz. Hal knew he would

have insisted on moving the bomb himself if he still had his glasses.

No one spoke. No one dared.

Boaz sat up, rubbing his hands together, working his fingers. He looked serenely calm. Taking hold of the end of the wire with the clips, he stretched it out so that it wouldn't get tangled, then he drew in a deep breath through his nose and his head disappeared into the hole.

Hal's heart was beating so hard it hurt. His breath came in tight gasps. He felt Marianne's grip tighten. Time seemed to slow. The sound of the train faded, and all Hal could hear was the blood pounding in his ears. His eyes were fixed on Boaz's back. It occurred to him that it might be the last thing he ever saw.

Except, he trusted Boaz. The world needed Boaz. This couldn't be the end of his story, or Marianne's, or Hal's.

Uncle Nat's face showed signs of effort as he pinned Boaz's calves to the floor of the carriage. Rising gracefully like the unfurling neck of a swan, Boaz pulled his chest up using his core muscles. His eyes, with laser-beam focus, were fixed on what he held in his hands. Brown-red sticks, bound with tape and wire: a package about the size of a bag of flour. It was the bomb.

With a dart of relief, Hal realized Boaz had broken the connection to the dynamo and the bomb hadn't exploded.

'Our battery's working!' he gasped.

With the strength and poise of a dancer, Boaz turned and placed the bomb on the tray. As soon as he'd let go,

Uncle Nat grabbed his arm and pulled him back on to his knees.

They stared at the tray, loaded with sticks of dynamite.

'I don't know how long we've got.' Boaz's voice was hoarse and he was trembling from the effort of moving the bomb. 'The watch batteries aren't strong and we have no idea how run-down they are.'

'I'll take the tray,' Hal said.

'Hal, no.' Uncle Nat got to his feet. 'It should be me.'

'You don't have your glasses,' Hal pointed out. 'You might trip.'

'But . . .' Uncle Nat spluttered.

'You're too late,' Boaz said.

Turning, Hal saw Marianne holding the tray out in front of her, walking calmly and carefully away from them. He ran after her, darting around her when she reached the lounge. He shoved furniture out of her way and held the door open as she approached.

She had the serene focus of a tightrope-walker. One foot wrong and they'd all fall.

With Hal going before her to clear away any obstacles, Marianne made her way to the rear carriage.

Uncle Nat and Boaz overtook them, hailing the truck. Boaz shouted out what he wanted Glen, the driver, to do. Glen saluted and did a handbrake turn, reversing onto the track. The other ute, driven by Josh, accelerated, pushing the bumper of Glen's truck towards the carriage.

Dropping to the floor, Boaz and Uncle Nat quickly fed

the metal sheet out till it rested on the tailgate of the truck.

Without a word, Marianne walked on to it.

Hal sent up a silent prayer, begging the wind outside to hold its breath as he held his own.

Kneeling, Marianne carefully shifted one knee forward, then another, holding the tray before her. 'Hold my feet,' she shouted.

Uncle Nat held down one of her ankles, and Boaz grabbed the other.

Marianne stretched forward, reaching out as far as she could as she lowered herself onto her stomach. She was holding the tray over the trailer, but her arms weren't long enough to place it safely onto the truckbed. Wiggling forward, centimetre by centimetre, she worked her way closer. As she got further and further away, Boaz and Uncle Nat struggled to hold on to her ankles and the metal sheet.

Stepping into the doorway, Hal dropped to all fours, taking hold of Marianne's calves.

Feeling his secure grip on her legs, Marianne rippled forward, and, as if she were holding a newborn baby in her arms, gently placed the tray into the trailer.

The moment the tray was down, Marianne recoiled, and Hal helped her back into the carriage. Boaz then drew back the metal sheet, and Uncle Nat shouted and waved for Glen to drive.

Knowing the dangerous load he was carrying, Glen allowed the truck to roll to a slower speed, then carefully steered the ute over the rails at a snail's pace.

As the truck cleared the rails and made it onto the dirt, Glen's head ducked down, and Hal heard the vroom of acceleration. The driver's door opened. Glen rolled out on to the ground as the truck sped off over the red dirt.

'He must have jammed the accelerator down,' said Boaz, as the third truck driver, Josh, drove over and picked him up.

The ute carrying the bomb careered over shrubs, getting further and further away. Hal couldn't take his eyes off it. *How long would their homemade battery last?* The truck bounced over a rocky patch of ground and suddenly there was a flash of light, an earth-thundering *KABOOM!* and the red ute rocketed into the air in a ball of flame, its doors spinning off.

Hal flinched back from the explosion.

'Crikey!' Boaz exclaimed.

'I didn't believe the bomb was real,' Marianne whispered.

Uncle Nat had collapsed to his knees, his head in his hands. 'That was too close.'

'We're OK, Uncle Nat.' Hal put a hand on his shoulder and suddenly felt weak. 'We did it. The bomb is gone!'

'All we have to do now is stop the train before it derails,' Boaz said, almost sounding like he was enjoying himself.

'How are you going to do that?' Uncle Nat asked, looking up.

'I've got a feeling you're not going to like it.' Boaz winced. 'I'm going to blow it apart, with hydrogen.'

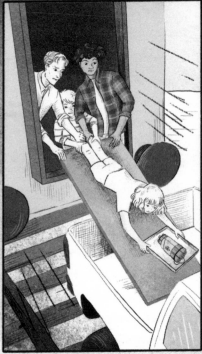

KABOOM

CHAPTER TWENTY-FIVE

MISSION: IMPOSSIBLE

'Before you freak out, let me explain.' Boaz held his hand up to silence Uncle Nat's protests. 'Underneath the train, there's a brake cable, right?' Uncle Nat nodded. 'The braking system is controlled by the computer, so we can't use it.' He held up his forefinger. 'However, when you join carriages together to form a train, they are connected by the coupling *and* the brake cable . . .' Uncle Nat's expression lightened as he realized the direction of Boaz's train of thought. 'And if you blow apart the brake cable . . .'

'The drop in air pressure will trigger the emergency braking system,' Uncle Nat finished his sentence.

Boaz nodded. 'The brakes on every carriage and the locomotive will be activated. We can stop the train before it hits the bend in the tracks through Karlu Karlu.' His eyes were dancing. 'We can save the Solar Express and *win*.'

'Wait, but *how* are you planning to blow the brake cable apart?'

'By making a teeny, tiny, controlled explosion,' Boaz replied.

'Then we'd better hurry up,' Marianne said, 'because we've got less than twenty minutes.'

'Let's go,' Boaz said, striding away.

'Where to?' Hal asked.

'The kitchen,' Boaz replied over his shoulder, 'and the switchboard. I need to get into the inverter box and change the electricity outlets from AC to DC. We're going to do some electrolysis.'

'Wait.' Uncle Nat hurried after them. 'I don't like the sound of an explosion. Surely there's another way?'

'If you can think of one, let's hear it,' Boaz said. But Uncle Nat couldn't.

With the bomb gone, Hal felt energized. He was determined to beat the saboteur and save the Solar Express.

Marianne had picked up Kira's camera and was looking as resolute as Hal felt. This was personal now.

In the kitchen, they lined up opposite Boaz.

'Listen up,' said Boaz. 'I need the largest plastic containers you can find – the bigger the better. And they must have lids. Got it?'

'Got it.' Hal and Marianne nodded as Uncle Nat began hunting through the cupboards.

'We're going to make electrodes,' Boaz continued. 'Normally I'd use flat metal plates, because they conduct electricity and have a big surface area, so I'm thinking fish slices or spatulas – anything made of stainless steel.'

Marianne was already scanning the scattered utensils on the kitchen floor.

'What about whisks?' She bent down and picked one up. 'There are loads of them.' She grabbed up a couple more, then ran to the sink. 'And we can stuff them with these.' She grabbed a stainless-steel scouring pad and pushed it through the bars of the whisk. 'It'll increase the surface area.' She slid the spacer disc down to trap the scouring pad in its whisk cage. Pushing down the metal sleeve of the hollow whisk handle, she said, 'And look, the hollow cylinder of the handle makes a gas outlet.'

'That's perfect,' Boaz said. 'Now I'm going to need an electrolyte to add to the water and make it more conductive.'

'A what? To do what?' Hal asked, wishing he knew more science.

'I need something ionic. Drain cleaner's good.' Boaz opened the cupboard below the sink. 'Na, nothing in there.' He scratched his head, then his expression brightened. 'Baking soda would work!'

'This enough?' Marianne was stood behind him holding a massive tin of baking soda.

'Yeah.' Boaz laughed. 'Now, what are we going to collect the gas in?' Boaz slowly turned on the spot as he thought. 'Ideally it would be some kind of canister that we can pressurize . . .'

'Fire extinguisher!' Hal yelled, pointing at one attached to the wall beside the stove.

'You beaut,' Boaz said, taking it out of its clips and examining the nozzle attachment. 'I think I can make this work. Hal, will you empty this into the sink for me?'

'Boaz, have you thought this through?' Uncle Nat asked, putting three large Tupperware containers on to the countertop that the caterers had used for the sushi. 'It's very hard to control an explosion.'

'Yup. I know,' Boaz replied as he opened cupboard doors. 'But—'

'Look, normally, when I split water into hydrogen and oxygen, I don't want the gases to mix. I collect the gases separately. Know why I do that? Because if there's only one output from the electrolysis unit, the gases mix, and you get the mixture oxyhydrogen. It's really explosive. One spark and *kerblammo*!'

'That's what I'm worried about,' Uncle Nat replied. 'We only just got a bomb *off* this train.'

'Train's still gonna derail if we don't stop it,' Boaz said bluntly. 'And we are stuck on it, with no way off.'

'Yes, but, there are tanks of hydrogen on this train, and the solar panels on the roof are constantly generating electricity . . .'

'I know. I designed them.'

'I'm finished,' Marianne called out. She had lined up four whisks of varying sizes on the countertop, each stuffed with scourers. 'What else do we need?'

Boaz turned away from Uncle Nat. 'We need tubes – something to feed the gas into and out of the compressor. It could be a thin hose or . . .'

There was silence as they all thought.

'The plumbing in the bathrooms?' suggested Uncle Nat. 'Plastic tubing delivers the water to the taps.'

'Great idea!' Boaz replied. 'Get me all the tubing you can.'

Uncle Nat looked as if he were going to protest, but nodded and left.

Boaz kept closing his eyes and muttering. 'I can use the compressor from the refrigerator . . . I need a power source.' He stared at the plug sockets. 'Marianne, I'm going to need more hair clips if you have them.'

'On it!' Marianne ran out of the kitchen.

'Hal, go grab me the hammer and crowbar from the toolbox.'

Hal sprinted to the driver's cabin, grabbed the tools and sprinted back.

Boaz had his arms wrapped around the refrigerator and was walking it into the kitchen. He took the hammer from Hal and whacked at the back of the machine, then he used the crowbar to wrench a round thing off the back.

'Fill those two tubs with water?' Boaz pointed at the ones Uncle Nat had found.

Hal nodded and rushed to the sink. When he was done, Boaz grabbed a kitchen knife and made two holes in each lid.

'Now stir the baking soda into the water,' Boaz said, handing him a wooden spoon. 'We need it to be saturated with the stuff. Keep pouring it in until no more will dissolve.'

Uncle Nat came into the kitchen with an armful of white plastic tubing, his face a picture of anxiety. 'Boaz, can we just talk about the explosion—'

'Mate,' Boaz cut him off. 'Do you know what oxyhydrogen does when it explodes?' He paused, as Uncle Nat blinked, searching his brain for the answer. 'When oxyhydrogen explodes, it turns back into water. You've gotta trust me on this one.'

Uncle Nat was glancing at the scars on Boaz's arms with a concerned expression. 'Accidents happen.'

'Not today they won't,' Boaz replied.

'Please, Uncle Nat,' Hal said, 'let's save the Solar Express. We can do it. I know we can.'

'What about finding a way to detonate the explosive remotely?' Uncle Nat tried.

'Was gonna do that anyway. It'll be a really big bang. We're going to have to shelter at the other end of the train when it goes off.'

'OK,' said Uncle Nat, giving in but looking unhappy about it.

'Good on ya!' Boaz grinned, grabbing the crowbar from the counter. 'Go to the gangway connecting this carriage and the observation pod and prise up the floor with this. There's a slit where the gangway of the two carriages meet. We need a hole big enough to jam the fire extinguisher into, no bigger.'

Uncle Nat left as Marianne returned waving her washbag.

'Mind if I borrow your sketchbook, Hal?' Boaz asked. 'I need to show you what we're making.'

Hal placed it on countertop and Boaz took the pencil from behind his ear, explaining as he drew.

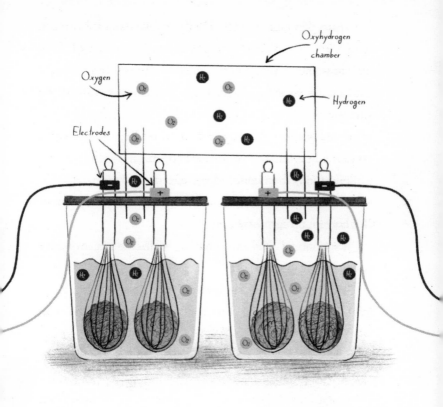

'The two tubs contain water and our electrolyte. Submerged in the water are two electrodes, one positive, one negative.' He drew the whisks. 'They produce hydrogen and oxygen bubbles that mix in the space above the water, and, because the gas is lighter than air, it rises up these tubes into this third container – the oxyhydrogen chamber.' He drew a box above the electrolysis tanks. 'Using the refrigerator compressor, I'm going to suck the gas from this chamber, compress it, and feed it through this hose into the fire extinguisher.' He tapped the fire extinguisher with his pen.

'The fire extinguisher is the bomb. All we have to do is set it off.'

'How are we going to do that?' Marianne asked.

'I'm still working on that part,' Boaz admitted, 'but we need to make as much gas as possible if this is going to work, so let's get going.'

Hal and Marianne each constructed an electrolysis tub while Uncle Nat wrangled with the tubing. Boaz pared back the ends of a piece of wire, took the covers off the plug sockets and hooked up each of the electrodes.

'It's working!' Hal exclaimed as both tubs began fizzing and bubbling.

Boaz powered up the compressor, attaching it to the

oxyhydrogen chamber and then the fire extinguisher. He stepped back.

'What's that noise?' Marianne asked, pricking up her ears. 'Is it the compressor?'

They all listened, hearing the raspberrying *VAROOM!* of a low-flying aircraft.

'No!' Boaz ran to the window, looking up. 'It's Ma!' he shouted, punching the air.

CHAPTER TWENTY-SIX

THE GREAT ESCAPE

Sprinting to the front of the train, they heard a roaring sound as Marlee's aircraft, with *Royal Flying Doctor Service* emblazoned across its body, swooped low over the top of the train, before banking off to one side in a high curve. Uncle Nat ran in behind them, still clutching the crowbar.

'That was Ma getting our attention,' Boaz said, a broad smile on his face.

Hal glanced at the speedometer and gasped. 'We're travelling at two hundred kilometres an hour!'

'Quick – into the engine room!' Boaz said, darting through the gap in the panelling, and going to the iron-rung ladder in the corner. Climbing up, he slid back a bolt and pushed up the hatch at the top. The wind caught it and flung it open with a *klang*.

Boaz poked his head out, and waved frantically to his mum, his hair blowing back from his face. The plane stopped climbing and levelled out, flying well ahead of the train.

'What's she doing?' Hal asked from the foot of the ladder.

'I don't know . . . Oh, wait. The door is opening! It's Koen!'

'How can you tell from this far away?' Marianne said.

'I'd know my brother from any distance,' Boaz replied. 'But Koen loves to skydive. He's won competitions. And he always wears bright pink.'

'What's he doing?' Uncle Nat asked.

'He's jumped!' Boaz whooped. 'He's holding on to something.' He ducked his head back inside and hopped off the ladder. 'He's carrying parachutes! They're trying to get us off the train.'

'But we're on the ground.' Marianne said.

'Crawl out there wearing one –' Boaz pointed up to the trapdoor – 'open the parachute, and . . . *whomp!* We're going that fast the wind'll drag you up off the train. Then you float to the ground.'

'But we don't need to get off the train,' Hal said. 'We're going to stop it.'

'We're also going to set off an oxyhydrogen explosive on it,' Uncle Nat pointed out.

'If we can get off the train before we blow it up, then we should,' Boaz agreed, and Hal saw for the first time that he was nervous about his plan not working. 'We need to catch those parachutes when Koen drops them.' Boaz hooked one foot and one arm around the ladder rungs and climbed as far he could, his back to the wind. His hair whipped about furiously.

Uncle Nat climbed up the other side of the ladder, squeezing out of the trapdoor beside Boaz. 'If the chute falls that way, you grab it and I'll hold on to you. If it falls this way, I'll grab it and you hold on to me.' They nodded at each other. Then Uncle Nat looked down the hole. 'You two hold on to our legs.'

'Got it!' Hal shouted, as he and Marianne moved to the foot of the ladder.

'Koen's ahead of us,' Boaz called out. 'He's opened his chute. He's got really good aim. Nine times out of ten he can hit a drop zone dead centre . . . but the drop zone has never been a moving train before.'

'We're catching up to him fast,' Uncle Nat shouted. 'Get ready. He's directly above the tracks.'

'NOW!' Boaz shouted.

Hal heard a terrifying *THUNK!* Then a second *THUNK!* Uncle Nat cried out. There was a series of bangs. Boaz and Uncle Nat were thrashing and shouting to each other. Hal and Marianne held tightly on to their calves and ankles.

'We got one,' Uncle Nat said, climbing down as Hal released his ankles. 'The other one has fallen down the side of the loco – it's stuck on the running board.'

'This chute is too big to get through the trapdoor,' Boaz said.

'Why are there only two?' Marianne exclaimed.

'They're tandem chutes,' Uncle Nat replied. 'Two people per chute.'

Boaz fastened the parachute to the roof of the train with the belt from his shorts. 'That's not going anywhere.'

'We're running out of time to stop the train,' Marianne fretted. 'Boaz, how are you going to set off the fire-extinguisher explosion?'

'Good question.' Boaz scratched his head. 'I need to make a fuse.' His pencil dropped from behind his ear, clattering to the floor.

Hal picked it up. 'What about a wooden one?' He held up the pencil.

'Not a bad idea!' Boaz grinned, taking it. 'I could coat the rubber bung with something flammable . . .'

'I've got nail polish in my washbag,' Marianne suggested. 'That burns like crazy.'

'I'll split the pencil in half, remove the lead, stab it into the bung, cover the bung and base with nail polish, and light the other end.' He nodded to himself as he thought this through. 'The rubber will burn and the moment the pressurized oxyhydrogen meets the burning rubber . . .' He made an exploding sound.

'You three are terrifying,' Uncle Nat whispered, shaking his head.

'How much time will that give us to get off the train?' Marianne asked.

'Three or four minutes,' Boaz replied, looking uncertain. 'I think.'

'Right, I'll help Boaz set up the fuse,' Marianne said. 'Mr Bradshaw, Hal, you get the second chute.'

'I think I can reach it,' Uncle Nat said to Hal, 'if I can find something to hook it with.'

'Bobby Benson's walking stick!' Hal cried, sprinting down the train.

As he passed through the dining car, Marianne shouted to him: 'We've seven minutes before the train derails! Once you've got the parachute, *go*! We're nearly done here.'

Hal grabbed the hooked wooden stick and scrambled back to Uncle Nat, who'd drawn back the bolts of the door in the wall of the loco and was heaving it open.

'Don't come out of this door unless I say so,' Uncle Nat instructed Hal, as he handed over the stick.

His uncle hooked the stick over his shoulder, trapping the shaft under his armpit. Then he stepped out on to the running board and grabbed the handrail. Keeping his back pressed against the engine to stop the wind from hurling him off the train, he edged along the narrow walkway.

Hal's heart was in his mouth. The noise of the train was deafening. Land was zipping by at a nauseating speed. He watched as Uncle Nat closed in on the parachute, a large black rucksack with lots of straps. Taking the stick in his left hand, Uncle Nat hooked it through a handle on the bag, yanking it towards him, then stamped his foot on it to hold it steady. Then, discarding the stick, he carefully crouched down, grabbed hold of the parachute and quickly worked his way back to Hal.

'Got it!' he gasped triumphantly.

In the shelter of the doorway, Uncle Nat strapped the

parachute to his back, handing a harness to Hal. 'Put that on. It attaches here and here at my shoulders, and here and here at my hips. 'Your back will be against my chest. I'm in control of the chute, you don't have to do anything except what I say. OK?'

Hal nodded, making sure his sketchbook was safe in his pocket before stepping into the harness.

'We need to be on the roof of the train to open the chute.' Uncle Nat pointed out of the door to a ladder of iron rungs scaling the locomotive. 'But we have to clip our harnesses together here. I may not be able to manage it up there. We'll be climbing as one.'

'OK,' Hal said, turning his back to his uncle so he could clip them together.

Marianne came running up the corridor with Kira's camera in one hand. 'Boaz has lit the fuse! Go! Go! *Go!*'

Uncle Nat and Hal sidled along the walkway, their combined weight making it easier to resist the pull of the wind. Reaching the ladder, Hal found climbing more difficult. He put his feet in the middle of the rungs, so Uncle Nat could use the outside.

'UP!' shouted Uncle Nat, as they rose in unison.

When their heads poked up above the train, the force of the wind was undeniable. Hal's mind fizzed with terror as he clung on, gripping the ladder so hard he couldn't feel his fingers.

'Keep climbing,' Uncle Nat shouted. 'We need to be higher!'

Hal stared at his hands, telling them to let go so he could climb, but they didn't.

Boaz's head and arms rose out of the trapdoor in the engine room. It was obvious from the speed at which he strapped the parachute on, and then attached it to Marianne, that he'd done it before.

'Hal! Let go!' Uncle Nat shouted. 'NOW!'

Boaz had lit the fuse. Any second now, an explosion would rip through the train.

Let go, you idiot! he ordered himself, and slowly his fingers uncurled.

Uncle Nat heaved them on to the roof, rolling them on to their sides. They started to slide, but Hal grabbed on to a vent to hold them steady.

'Curl your knees into your chest. We're going to get onto all fours,' barked Uncle Nat as he grabbed a handle on the roof with both hands. 'You under me.' Hal moved with his uncle until they were crouching on the roof of the train. 'On three, we're going to jump up with all our might,' Uncle Nat shouted. 'One . . . two . . . THREE!'

Hal pushed his hands and feet against the train, leaping up as Uncle Nat pulled the ripcord and the parachute opened, yanking them up, inflating with the train's slipstream.

Below them, the train rocketed forward at two hundred kilometres an hour. In the distance, Hal could see the railway track snaking around some large rocks. Uncle Nat pointed at Boaz, who had his arm around Marianne's waist.

He pulled his ripcord, and Hal felt his spirits lift as the pair sailed up above the receding Solar Express.

'Bend your knees,' Uncle Nat shouted, and Hal suddenly saw that the ground was hurtling towards him.

They landed in a bundle on red dust just as an earth-shattering *BOOM!* made the two middle carriages of the Solar Express buck like mules, blasting apart with a flash of light.

Hal saw the floating figures of Boaz and Marianne punch the air as the brakes of the Solar Express stopped the wheels with a deafening squeal. Sparks flew as the whole train juddered and ground to a halt five hundred metres away from them.

'By George!' Uncle Nat whispered. 'He did it!'

'I knew he would,' Hal said, hugging his uncle with delight.

Marianne and Boaz landed, their parachute falling on top of them, and the growl of the aeroplane made Hal look up. Marlee was landing.

Uncle Nat unclipped their harnesses. Hal heard a shout and saw Koen running towards them. Seconds later, Marianne and Boaz were bounding over, whooping, and talking ten to the dozen.

'We saved the Solar Express!' Marianne said, her eyes shining.

'We saved Karlu Karlu!' Hal exclaimed.

'Of course,' Boaz said flatly. 'Never doubted we would.' He drew himself up, and in an almost perfect impersonation of August Reza, said, 'The future's in good hands, don't you think, Nathaniel?'

Hal laughed, finding this absurdly funny, and then they were all laughing, with relief and exhaustion, till there were tears on their cheeks and they had to hold their sides.

CHAPTER TWENTY-SEVEN
FACE/OFF

Marlee marched each of them onto her plane, one by one, insisting on checking them for injuries, concussion, or signs of shock. They were tired, and had a few cuts and bruises, but euphoric at having outsmarted the saboteur.

Afterwards, they sat on the ground grinning at the Solar Express. Koen handed out bottles of water, and Uncle Nat complimented him on his skills with a parachute. Marlee scolded Boaz for staying on the train, while simultaneously brimming with pride.

'Boaz Tudawali,' Marianne said, training Kira's camera on him as he sat on the plane's steps. 'How does it feel to have saved Karlu Karlu from the evil plotting of the Solar Express saboteur?'

'You tell me,' Boaz replied. 'Couldn't have done it without ya.'

'Look.' Hal pointed to the dust dancing on the rail tracks, bouncing as the metal vibrated. 'Something's coming.'

'Pop!' Marianne cried out, as the NR3 appeared in the

distance, reversing towards them. Hal realized that, even though she hadn't let on, she must've been worrying about him the whole time.

Beside the diesel locomotive drove a red ute, in the back of which Hal could make out Kira, Michelle and Vincent, with JJ in his arms. Behind them were two police cars, and in the distance, he saw an approaching helicopter.

Taking a deep breath, Hal put his hand into his pocket and patted his sketchbook. He knew what he had to do.

The NR3 stopped beside the plane, and August came hurtling out on to the running board, jumping down to the ground to pick Marianne up in a hug. Woody followed, pushing Terry Chang in front of him. There was a makeshift bandage around the bodyguard's head, stained with blood, and the business tycoon's wrists were bound with tape. Shamefaced, Leslie and Tom came out after them. The politician was looking sullen, and Tom was snivelling. Bobby Benson shuffled out behind them, making sure they couldn't run away.

'Oh! Woody!' Marianne exclaimed, breaking away from her father when she saw his injury. 'Are you OK?'

Woody nodded.

Marianne pointed Kira's camera at Terry Chang. 'Here are the mutinous cowards who attacked an innocent man and left children to die!' she declared dramatically.

'We didn't know there was a bomb on the train,' Leslie snapped.

'Would it have made any difference?' Marianne replied, and Leslie's pause spoke volumes.

Vincent handed JJ to Marlee, who'd sprinted to the truck as it stopped. She cuddled her daughter, tickling her and making her laugh.

Michelle and Kira stepped down from the ute, approaching the group. Tom tried to talk to Kira, but she walked straight past him, responding with a rude finger gesture, as the police cars parked, and two pairs of officers got out.

'I got lots of good footage,' Marianne said, handing her the camera. 'I filmed everything I could.'

'Thanks.' Kira grinned. 'When I make the documentary, I'll credit you as a camera operator if you like?'

'I'd love that!' Marianne replied.

'Where are Kenny and Karleen?' Hal asked, as Marianne began filling her father in on everything that had happened.

'Mandy drove them to the hospital in Alice Springs,' Michelle explained.

'When I find out who did this . . .' August was trying to contain his fury as Marianne finished her story.

'Would you like me to tell you who it was?' Hal asked quietly, and August's head jerked round to look at him.

'Yes,' he said. 'Very much so.'

Hal leaned in, whispering something to him. August nodded, hailing everyone to gather around.

'What's happening?' Boaz asked Marianne.

'You're going to want a ringside seat and a bag of popcorn,' Marianne replied, perching on the running board of the NR3.

Hal waited until August had everyone's attention, and then stepped forward. 'I know who sabotaged the train,' he said, pausing as everyone leaned forward except the saboteur, who stood stock-still. 'Officers, I'd like you to arrest Bobby Benson.'

There was a ripple of shock.

The police officers didn't move, and August frowned.

'Hal, you must be mistaken,' August whispered. 'Bobby was upset by the mutiny. He wasn't a part of it. He helped me, and drove the NR3 after the Solar Express. It wasn't him.'

'I don't mind,' Bobby Benson said with a chuckle. 'Let the boy play his game. We could do with a laugh after today's drama.'

'You don't know who this boy is, do you?' said Marianne, glaring at Bobby Benson, and Hal saw that Woody had sidestepped to stand behind the elderly man.

'As a matter of fact, I don't,' Bobby Benson admitted.

'He's the boy that's going to send you to prison,' Marianne snapped, but Hal could see that, other than Uncle Nat, she was the only person who believed him. Even Boaz was frowning.

'Tell us, Hal,' Uncle Nat prompted.

'Contact the hotel we stayed in, in Alice Springs,' Hal instructed the police officers. 'You'll find two rooms booked for tonight. One for Bobby Benson – which is strange, because we're all supposed to be arriving in Darwin this evening. The second room will be for a Mr G. Vulpes. In that room, you'll find the real Bobby Benson.' He pointed. 'This is not him.' Hal approached the elderly man. 'What did you do to Mr Benson? Drug him? Tie him to a chair?'

The old man wheezed out a laugh, looking around as if they should all be finding this funny, but no one was. They were all staring at him.

'Sir, please remove your wig or I'll ask Woody to do it for you.'

Woody didn't wait. He reached forward and yanked at the silver hair. It came away, along with a silicone-freckled balding pate, revealing slicked-back dark locks beneath.

'It's him!' Marianne yelled, almost falling off the NR3 in her excitement. 'He's shaved, but that's the man who delivered the Rocket model to Pop's hotel room!'

Everyone stared as the stranger straightened his posture, looking younger by the second. He peeled off his prosthetic nose, calm and defiant.

'Who the hell are you?' August Reza asked with a snarl.

The man's mouth turned up on one side. He spat on the ground, saying nothing.

'He's Professor Gregory Vulpes,' Hal said. 'He entered the Reza's Rocket competition with a design for a nuclear-powered train. He was furious that he didn't win, but became enraged when he saw that an Australian child had beaten him.'

Boaz stepped forward, taking a long look at Gregory Vulpes, and Kira trained her camera on them.

'How did you feel when you saw the worldwide media attention the Reza's Rocket competition was generating, Mr Vulpes?' Hal asked. 'Must've really stung.'

'*Professor* Vulpes to you, child,' the man snapped, dropping his phoney Australian accent.

'A fourteen-year-old beat you to the prize, and the world hails him a genius,' Hal said softly. 'That's got to hurt?'

'There's nothing clever about hydrogen. It's child's play. It'll never be efficient enough to power vehicles.'

'The man's a Pom!' Vincent muttered to Marlee, hearing his British accent.

'Then you had an idea. What if the Solar Express exploded, like the *Hindenburg*? The public would think hydrogen was unsafe. It could trigger the swing back to investment in nuclear power you so desire.' Hal saw the muscles around Gregory Vulpes's eyes twitch, and knew he was right. 'You decided to sabotage the train. But it wasn't enough. You wanted to *show* August Reza how clever you are, even if he wasn't smart enough to see. That's why you designed a puzzle box, based on the original Rocket locomotive, the one his competition was named after. You delivered it to his hotel door, certain that he would never find the message concealed inside: that the Solar Express would derail and explode. You even inserted a clue to your identity.' Hal took the gold fox from his pocket and held it up.

Mr Vulpes raised an eyebrow.

'I found this inside the barrel of the Rocket model that Marianne witnessed you leaving outside Mr Reza's hotel door. It's a gold fox. On three of its paws are the nuclear symbols for the hydrogen isotopes, and on the fourth are your own initials, GV, Gregory Vulpes – and in Latin, *Vulpes* means *fox*.'

'Why would he give himself away like that?' August asked, baffled.

'He didn't think you'd ever work out the puzzle box. He imagined it sitting on a shelf in your office, silently mocking you for years. That's the kind of arrogant man *Professor* Vulpes is. He thinks he's cleverer than you, Boaz – cleverer than all of us.'

'But . . . he tried to kill me?' August said.

'It wasn't his intention. Your plan went wrong, didn't it, Professor Vulpes?' Hal said.

Mr Vulpes opened his mouth to say something, but then glanced at the police officers, scowled, and snapped it shut.

'How about I tell you what I think happened, and you tell me the bits I get wrong?' Hal said. 'Yesterday you arrived at the hotel, accosted Bobby Benson, and took him and his suitcase hostage. You borrowed a porter's jacket and delivered the Rocket model. Then you went to Bobby's hotel room, and tried on his clothes and the prosthetics you'd brought with you. You knew about him because it was a big Australian news story that he'd been invited on the Solar Express. You took a trip down to reception to test out your disguise, to see if it would fool people, and it did.' Hal opened his sketchbook and showed Gregory Vulpes the sketch of him beside the reception desk. 'Unluckily for you, I was in the lobby, drawing. In this picture, you'll see that you're holding two room keys, and that you also don't have Mr Benson's walking stick.'

Several people gasped.

'This morning you got up, disguised yourself as Bobby Benson, went down to breakfast early, and waited for Francisco Silva, who'd agreed to give you a private tour of the Solar Express. You introduced yourself as the loveable train driver who'd dedicated his life to Australia's railways, and he took you to Alice Springs station. You probably asked questions about how it worked, getting all the information you needed from him to sabotage the train.'

Hal looked past Gregory to Woody. 'Could you check his pockets please, Woody?'

Woody did as Hal asked, and produced a black and orange plastic card, a penknife, and a plastic freezer bag containing a handkerchief.

'Francisco's key card!' August exclaimed.

'Yes, and I'd guess that that handkerchief is soaked in a chemical that will knock a person out,' Hal said as Woody passed the items to a police officer.

Professor Gregory Vulpes glared at Hal.

'If you've hurt Francisco . . .' August clenched his fists.

'I think he locked Francisco in a cupboard at the station,' Hal said, looking at Uncle Nat.

'Yes!' Uncle Nat cried. 'I heard banging as we boarded the train.'

'Nobody was alarmed by Mr Silva's disappearance, because he'd quarrelled with August the night before,' Hal continued. 'You'd planted the bomb before we boarded, but you had to wait until the train had left the station to do the rest, so you excused yourself by saying you needed the men's room.

Then you slipped into the driver's cabin, used Francisco's key card to reprogram the computer, and the knife to disable the manual override and the brakes.'

Michelle folded her arms across her chest, looking furious.

'I thought you said he didn't plan to kill us?' Vincent looked about ready to thump Mr Vulpes.

'The bomb wasn't meant to hurt anyone, just destroy the train,' Hal said. 'He thought, once you realized the train wasn't under your control, you'd abandon the Solar Express, and use the NR3 to go back to Alice Springs. He planned for the Solar Express to speed into Karlu Karlu, where it would derail on one of the bends and, the moment the wheels stopped turning, the bomb would detonate, blowing up the hydrogen tanks and creating a devastating explosion that would bury the Solar Express project and destroy Boaz's credibility and spirit.'

Vincent moved to stand beside his son, and they both looked ready to pounce on Professor Vulpes.

'But August and Boaz tried to save the Solar Express,' continued Hal. 'Disguised as Bobby, Professor Vulpes tried to persuade people that taking the NR3 back to Alice was the best course of action, but the group split when Kenny got hurt, triggering a mutiny led by Leslie Deane and Terry Chang. Mr Vulpes found himself marooned on the NR3, a slower locomotive than the Solar Express.' He turned to the saboteur. 'You must have known then that all hope of getting away with this was gone. You'd doomed innocent people to die, because you were too arrogant to accept that Boaz's train is a worthy winner.'

'Except we didn't die, and the Solar Express didn't explode.' Marianne grinned.

'Must be pretty gutting to have failed twice *and* got beaten by a bunch of kids, eh?' Boaz laughed.

'You underestimate children, Professor Vulpes,' Hal said. 'A child designed a better train than yours. A child spotted what you were up to when you delivered the Rocket model, which, together with my uncle, we solved. It was children working together who defused your bomb and stopped the Solar Express.' Hal stepped towards him. 'And this child is going to send you to prison.'

The sound of the approaching helicopter became deafeningly loud, stopping all talk. The red dust was lifted by the rotating blades and everyone shielded their eyes as the chopper landed.

Professor Vulpes broke away, kicking Woody in the shins, and making a run for it.

'Stop him!' Marianne howled, but the bodyguard was not about to let his quarry escape. He sprinted after him, hurling himself at Professor Vulpes's back, bringing him down to earth with a thud.

From the helicopter stepped Francisco Silva, his face marked with a black eye. He and August crossed the ground to embrace. Marianne ran to them, and Francisco kissed her forehead. They turned to look at Professor Vulpes, face down in the dirt, Woody's knee on his back.

'Officers!' August shouted. 'You heard Harrison Beck. Arrest that man!'

CHAPTER TWENTY-EIGHT

TRAINSPOTTING

Hal and Uncle Nat spent three days in Alice Springs with Marianne and August, helping the police with their enquiries. The real Bobby Benson had been discovered tied up to a hotel bed with an empty pizza box beside him and the TV on. He was confused and shaken, but otherwise OK. They'd visited Kenny in hospital and found him sitting up in bed with Karleen fussing around him.

'I'm a hero,' Kenny told them cheerfully when they arrived in his hospital room with fruit and chocolate. 'Says so on the news.'

'He's going to be just fine,' Karleen said, noticing Hal's concerned glances at Kenny's bandaged neck and arms. 'It's mostly first-degree burns, which will heal. The doctor said it's a very good job he was wearing glasses.'

August Reza had insisted on taking care of everyone who'd been caught up in the drama. As a gift, he'd bought Hal and Nat two Platinum Service tickets to travel on the Indian Pacific, crossing Australia from east coast to west, from

Sydney to Perth, before they had to fly home.

He'd brought in a burns specialist for Kenny and sent Michelle on holiday with the promise of a job on Francisco's team when she returned. Kira had asked August if he could help her make her documentary, and travelled to Sydney with her camera equipment, to a swanky edit suite, to meet the award-winning editor who was going to help her put her film together.

Tom had returned to England with his tail between his legs, knowing that the moment Kira's film came out, his career would be forever limited to local news, if he was lucky. Leslie Deane, too, knew her career in public office would soon be over, but as an apology to August Reza, she approved his application to lease land for clean hydrogen production. Terry Chang was initially charged with assault for hurting Woody, but he bargained hard with Reza Tech, offering to switch his entire fleet of ships to hydrogen power within the next ten years and the charges were dropped.

Marianne had promised Woody that she would never be mean to him ever again and asked her father to give him a pay rise and a promotion. August had been so impressed by his daughter's leadership skills that he'd suggested she pick a project to work on at the company, and she'd chosen the Solar Express. Marianne said she was determined to make the train a success for the future of the planet, but Hal suspected it might also have something to do with Boaz.

After visiting the Uterne Homestead one last time, and saying their goodbyes to Boaz and the Tudawalis, Hal and

Uncle Nat flew to Melbourne to get their holiday back on track. They travelled on the trams and visited the zoo, before journeying east to Belgrave to ride on a famous narrow-gauge steam railway called Puffing Billy.

The Puffing Billy locomotive was a cheerful bottle-green and pillarbox-red, NA class, tank engine. As Hal clambered aboard, he felt awash with comfort and pleasure to be on a steam train once again. The more he travelled, the more he knew his heart belonged to steam-powered locomotives. The carriages of Puffing Billy were open-sided, with protective railings, and passengers were allowed to sit on the window ledge, dangling their legs and arms under and over the bars.

Uncle Nat followed Hal onto the train, his nose in a pamphlet. 'Now, I don't want you to be alarmed, but it says

here that at its top speed, Puffing Billy can go thirty kilometres per hour!'

Hal laughed as he clambered up to sit on the window ledge. 'I wouldn't mind if we went at *five* kilometres an hour,' he said, drinking in every delightful detail of the redbrick station with its salmon-pink roof that provided a perch for a line of green gouldian finches. 'I am going to love every second of this journey.'

'We must look out for the fifteen-span Monbulk Creek trestle bridge. It's wonderfully old and rickety-looking.'

The whistle of the train tooted to warn passengers it was ready to depart, and Hal sighed happily, waving at the station master dressed in a navy three-piece suit and hat, a handbell in one hand and a flag in the other.

'Uncle Nat, we should be proper tourists and take a selfie.'

Uncle Nat laughed, lifting up his camera, which was hanging around his neck, and turned it around. They grinned merrily at it as he pressed the button.

'Before you took me travelling on trains, I didn't know water was so powerful,' Hal mused, as he watched the exhausted steam puffing out of the locomotive chimney. 'You heat water, turning it into steam, and it can power a steam train. If you use electrolysis to split water into hydrogen and oxygen, it can power the Solar Express.'

'Or blow apart its carriages,' Uncle Nat said, giving his head a slight shake as Hal grinned. 'What on earth are we going to tell your mother when we get home?' He removed his newly repaired glasses and wiped the lenses. 'I'm afraid she'll never let me see you again. I was so sure that this trip would be safe. I promised her it would be.'

'Mum will come round,' Hal said. 'She worries about me, but she's proud of me too. And she trusts you to look after me. Anyway, we can't not tell her – it's all over the news.'

'I played the drama down when I spoke to her on the phone.'

'But when Kira's film comes out . . .'

'We'll cross that bridge when we get to it.'

'But we *will* go on another train adventure, won't we?'

'Actually, I have something in mind for Christmas, but I'll have to beg your mum for permission first.'

'Oh! Where to? On what train?'

Uncle Nat laughed. 'You'll just have to wait and see.'

A NOTE FROM
THE AUTHORS

Dear Reader,

This story is inspired by our favourite action movies, real-life science and the glorious country of Australia. Like all action movies, much of it is improbable, even if possible, and of course we've played hard and fast with reality in places to make it a thrilling read. We'd like to invite you into our engine room to show you what has inspired us and where we've tinkered with the truth.

The Ghan

The Ghan is one of Australia's most famous trains. Originally it was hauled by steam locomotives that refilled their tanks using water towers drawing from the Great Artesian Basin.

Construction of the railway line from Adelaide (on the south coast of Australia) began in 1878. It took fifty years for the tracks to reach north to Alice Springs. The project was beset with problems – termites chewed through sleepers and floods washed them away. Passengers would sometimes have to disembark and help repair damaged track. One train arrived three months late! In 1980 the route of The Ghan was changed to a safer one. The new line extended from Alice Springs to Darwin (on the north coast of Australia). It was finished in 2004 – over a hundred years after construction began.

Puffing Billy and the Indian Pacific
Puffing Billy is a Victorian narrow-gauge heritage railway outside Melbourne, and one of the most popular in the world. The Indian Pacific is over a hundred years old and the second longest train journey in the world, after the Trans-Siberian Railway. It takes four days and passes through three time zones as the train crosses Australia, from Perth to Sydney.

Stephenson's Rocket
One of the most famous locomotives in the world is Stephenson's Rocket. It was built and won the Rainhill Trails in 1829, becoming the first steam engine to pull the passenger trains along the Liverpool and Manchester Railway. The design of Rocket was utilized across the entire railway network, becoming an iconic symbol of the Industrial Revolution.

Powering Vehicles
Trains are the greenest form of public transport we have. They are terrifically efficient: riding a diesel train is better for the planet than driving a petrol-powered car.

As well as petrol, diesel, electricity and hydrogen, vehicles can be fuelled by ethanol, cooking oil and other things. In 1941, Henry Ford, the inventor of the world's first motor car, showcased a car that was made from and powered by plants. There's even a bus in Bristol powered by poo! Being creative about the fuels we burn is going to be an important way of dealing with climate change.

Hydrogen fuel cells are used to power cars, forklift trucks, motorcycles and some London buses. They have gradually become an alternative to petrol, diesel or battery power, but right now, they are not as energy-efficient.

Hydrogen Power

The most efficient way to power a train is with electrified overhead cables. However, most of the world's railways have not been electrified. Trains on these lines must use other fuels – usually diesel. Hydrogen is a replacement fuel that is cleaner and greener than diesel, particularly when it's made using renewable energy.

A small number of hydrogen trains already exist. A hydrogen-powered passenger train has been running in Germany since 2018. In 2021, at the COP26 climate summit in Glasgow, we were invited by Network Rail to ride the UK's first hybrid hydrogen train, the HydroFLEX.

The Tudawali RFC

We have used creative licence to enable Boaz to have discovered a catalyst that makes an efficient regenerative hydrogen fuel cell that could power a locomotive like the Solar Express.

Sadly, no such regenerative fuel cell exists, but it could do.

Regenerative fuel-cell power systems are used and being developed by NASA for lunar and Martian surface exploration. However, the technology has limitations which make it unable to compete with the efficiency of the fuels we use here on Earth.

Hydrogen is an explosive gas and can be very dangerous. **PLEASE DO NOT TRY ANY OF BOAZ'S EXPERIMENTS AT HOME. SCIENTIFIC EXPERIMENTS SHOULD ALWAYS BE DONE WITH A GROWN-UP PRESENT, USING PROPER SAFETY PRECAUTIONS.**

Solar Power in Australia

A real solar-powered passenger train exists in Australia, running on a short section of track in Byron Bay. When the sun isn't shining, it runs on electrical power from the national grid, or can be fuelled by diesel. It is the world's first solar-powered train.

The world's largest solar farm is being built in Australia between Alice Springs and Darwin, covering about 120 square kilometres, and is expected to generate ten gigawatts of renewable electricity – enough to power several million homes.

Lithium Batteries

Rechargeable batteries store energy. Lithium is used in rechargeable lithium-ion batteries. These batteries power electric cars and some trains. They reduce our reliance on fossil fuels. However, lithium mining can cause harm. Aboriginal communities in Australia have raised objections to the large tracts of land which have been destroyed to dig up lithium. Lithium-ion batteries get weaker over time until they can no longer be used. Safely disposing of used lithium-ion batteries is complex and expensive, and can create toxic by-products.

Nuclear-powered trains

Gregory Vulpes's idea for a nuclear-powered train is not new. We have nuclear-powered submarines, which were first constructed in the 1950s, and the 'atomic train' was a proposed vehicle in this period that has been regularly revisited because of its ability to travel great distances without the need for refuelling.

In some ways, we already have nuclear trains: the electricity which powers trains in many countries is generated at nuclear power stations.

Find Out More . . .

If you'd like to learn more about the railways of the world, Sam has written a fantastic non-fiction book called *Epic Adventures*, exploring the world through twelve amazing train journeys. It is beautifully illustrated by Sam Brewster and combines incredible maps with amazing facts.

Visit **adventuresontrains.com** to learn about Hal's other adventures, for videos, drawing and other activities and classroom resources.

ACKNOWLEDGEMENTS

This book was assembled at breakneck speed, and we have a great many people to thank for ensuring that no necks were actually broken during its construction.

Elisa Paganelli has outdone herself, yet again, bringing Hal's drawings to life with such imagination, skill, and at an eye-watering speed. We love you, Elisa. We are so grateful to have you on board. You turn our stories into something special, and we are always amazed when we see your work.

We are tremendously grateful to every member of Team Trains at Macmillan: Sarah Hughes, Sarah Plows, Rachel Vale, Jo Hardacre, as well as Sam, Alyx, Charlie, Amy, Nick de Somogyi, and the many others who work so hard to keep this series under steam. And to Brianne Collins for making sure we represented an authentic Australia.

Thank you to Kirsty McLachlan, our sterling agent, who is always in our corner.

Thank you to Sam Harmsworth Sparling for taking care of both of us.

We'd like to thank Jana Sparks and the team at Network Rail

for inviting us to the COP26 climate conference in Glasgow for a ride on the HydroFLEX, the UK's first hydrogen train. It was magical to meet Helen Simpson, inventor and engineer of the HydroFLEX, who was so helpful in answering our many queries about fuel cells and the specifics of Australian coupling mechanisms.

To all the booksellers, teachers, librarians and parents who have championed our stories and recommended them to readers: we thank you.

M. G. Leonard

I am not a scientist, but I am lucky enough to have a great friend who is. I owe a debt of gratitude to Dr Simon Jones, whom I affectionally call Lloydy, for talking to me about hydrogen fuel cells and reading an early draft of this book. I want to thank my son Sebastian and my husband Sam for going through the nuts and bolts of plot points over dinner with me, and my other son Arthur, who along with the rest of our family has put up with having an absent mum. I want to wave across the globe at my friend Karleen Harrington, a divinely inspiring Australian.

Thank you to my co-author, Sam Sedgman, who got me to watch many action movies in preparation for writing this story and made the process of creating this book a lot of fun.

Sam Sedgman

I must thank my parents, who once organized a legendary family holiday to Australia where I rode my first ever sleeper train, from Brisbane to Cairns. Thank you for inspiring me, and always being there to support me and champion my work. Dad, I am sorry there aren't more termite mounds in this book; I know how much you love them.

Thank you, of course, to Maya: the greatest person I know to blow up trains with, and to her husband Sam, who does so much to keep us both from losing the plot.

A big thank you to my housemates Bob, Kim and Roisin for all the support, camaraderie, booze, hugs, friendship and hot meals an author could want. And a special thanks to my friend Ciara, a wonderful neighbour, camera operator and Australian correspondent. I hope you liked your pigtails.

ABOUT THE
AUTHORS

M. G. Leonard has made up stories since she was a girl, but back then adults called them lies or tall tales and she didn't write them down. As a grown-up, her favourite things to create stories about are beetles, birds and trains. Her books have been translated into over forty languages and won many awards. She is the vice president of the insect charity Buglife, and a founding author of Authors4Oceans. She lives in Brighton with her husband, two sons, a fat cat called Kasper, a dog called Nell, and a variety of exotic beetles.

Sam Sedgman is a bestselling author and presenter. Before writing stories for children, he worked as playwright, journalist, and digital producer, and founded a company making murder mystery treasure hunts for adventurous Londoners. Written with his friend, M. G. Leonard, *The Highland Falcon Thief* was Sam's first book for young readers. A lifelong fan of puzzles, games, and detective fiction, he grew up with a railway at the bottom of his garden and has been mad about trains ever since. He lives in London.

THE
ARCTIC
RAILWAY
ASSASSIN

Coming in October 2022